Stories to Share with My Partner

Book 12

Camden Books Publishing

José F. Nodar

Stories to Share with My Partner Book 5 / José F. Nodar
ISBN: 978-0-9756618-5-7 - Paperback
ISBN: 978-1-76377054-6-3 - E-Book

Dedication

In loving memory of my wife,

Miriam Vassallo Nodar,

and her enduring presence.

You are always in my thoughts.

For anyone who's ever loved deeply, lost fully, and still found

the courage to begin again.

Table of Contents

Once Upon A Crime

In the bustling metropolis of Northport, New South Wales, there was a detective agency run by none other than Basil "Buzzy" Burton, a man so unlucky he once tripped over his own shadow. He prided himself on solving cases that nobody else wanted, mostly because those cases had already been solved, and he was just bad at keeping up with the news.

Buzzy's office was on the third floor of an aging building wedged between a questionable sandwich shop and a pet store that exclusively sold animals missing at least one limb. Business wasn't great, but Buzzy was a glass-half-full kind of guy, mostly because his landlord had taken the other half of the glass as rent.

One day, as he was practicing his "thinking pose" in front of his cracked mirror, the office door flew open with the grace of an elephant on roller skates. In walked a woman straight out of a noir film, wearing a red dress, heels sharp enough to commit assault, and eyes that could melt an ice cube at twenty paces.

"Mr Burton, I need your help," she said, a voice like honey with a side of bourbon. "My name is Veronica Nightshade. My husband has been murdered."

Buzzy, ever the professional, responded by choking on his own coffee. "Murdered, you say? Are you sure? Maybe he just took a really deep nap?"

"He was found in our study, slumped over his desk with a dagger in his back and a note pinned to his collar that read, 'I murdered him. Signed, The Murderer.'"

"Ah. Yes. That does sound murder-y."

Veronica let out a dramatic sigh.

"The police think it was me, Detective. They say it's always the spouse. But I loved my husband despite his terrible taste in jazz music and his insistence on putting tomato sauce on steak. I need you to clear my name!"

"Don't worry, Mrs Nightshade," Buzzy said, pulling out a notepad that had grocery lists scribbled in the margins. "I'll sort this out! Right after I figure out what happened to my pen."

The Nightshade residence was the kind of place that made you feel poor just by looking at it. Chandeliers the size of compact cars, gold-trimmed everything, and a door attendant who sneezed into a silk handkerchief with a monogrammed 'N.' Buzzy adjusted his tie (which he had borrowed from his neighbour's laundry line) and walked inside.

The study was exactly as Veronica had described, except for one detail. The dagger was gone. In its place, someone had left a Post-it note with a smiley face drawn on it. A mocking, crime-scene-defiling smiley face.

Buzzy rubbed his chin as he had seen real detectives do. "Interesting."

"What is it?" Veronica asked.

"Oh, nothing. I just say that when I do not know what's going on." He looked around. "Who found the body?"

"Our butler, Reginald. He's been with the family for years. He once killed a man with a spoon."

Buzzy blinked. "I feel like that should have been mentioned sooner."

Reginald was a tall, stiff man who looked like he had been born wearing a suit. When questioned, he gave clipped, efficient answers, unless asked about the spoon incident, at which point he waxed poetic about leverage and pressure points.

"Did you touch the murder weapon?" Buzzy asked.

"No, sir. I have been framed before, and I do not care for it."

"Understandable. Anyone else in the house that night?"

"The chef, the gardener, and Mr Nightshade's accountant. The chef was in the kitchen making a five-course meal for the house cat, the gardener was trimming the hedge into a topiary of a disgruntled walrus, and the accountant was doing, well, accounting things."

Buzzy scribbled nonsense in his notebook. "And where is the murder weapon now?"

"Gone, sir. Vanished without a trace."

Buzzy narrowed his eyes. "Then I have only one theory."

"Oh?" Veronica leaned in.

"Your house is haunted."

There was a long silence.

"Mr Burton," Veronica said slowly, "perhaps we should explore more rational explanations?"

"Fine, fine. Rational. Boring. But fine. The butler said that the chef had made a meal for the cat. Let's interrogate the cat."

Buzzy found the feline in question, a bloated Persian named Sir Luddington, lounging on a velvet cushion like an aristocrat who had lost a duel but still kept his dignity. Buzzy knelt before him. "Sir Luddington, what do you know about the murder?"

The cat blinked once, then slowly knocked Buzzy's notepad off the table.

"Aha! A clue!" Buzzy declared.

Veronica pinched the bridge of her nose. "He does that to everything."

"Exactly! He's covering something up."

At that moment, the front door slammed open. A tall and lanky man in a ski mask ran through the hallway, clutching a dagger and screaming, "I AM THE MURDERER! I HAVE RETURNED FOR DRAMATIC EFFECT!"

Everyone stared.

The intruder blinked. "Uh. I should not have said that aloud."

Reginald tackled him to the ground with the swiftness of a man who had definitely killed with a spoon before.

The police arrived, and as they dragged the would-be murderer away, Buzzy dusted off his hands. "Well, another case solved!"

Veronica shook her head in disbelief. "I suppose I should thank you?"

"No need. Just doing my job. If you ever need more detecting done, you know where to find me!"

She looked at him. "Where, exactly?"

"Good question. I should probably get business cards."

As he strolled out of the mansion, whistling a tune he didn't know the name of, Buzzy felt satisfied.

Sure, a cat had nearly outsmarted him, accused a ghost, and gotten lucky with a confession, but in the world of private detecting, that still counted as a win.

And for Buzzy Burton, that was more than enough.

A Tale of Two Flights

I know airport waiting areas are typically sterile, silent ecosystems fuelled by weak coffee and simmering resentment, but the Melbourne domestic terminal that morning was different.

It was 6:00 a.m., and the air felt thick with the low-grade chaos of a hundred Melburnians attempting to process a flight before their first proper coffee.

I was slumped in a moulded plastic chair at Gate 42, waiting for Qantas Flight QF437, bound for Sydney, and trying to ignore the aggressive pop music leaking from the nearby souvenir shop.

Then, the static hit.

It was the specific ear-splitting sound of a microphone being handled by someone who fundamentally distrusted volume levels.

"Good morning, valued passengers," a voice, clearly reading from a script marked 'Maximum Sincerity,' boomed across the entire concourse. This was Ms. Penelope, our Qantas gate agent. "This is an important update regarding Qantas service, Flight QF437 to Sydney. We regret to inform you with a deep and profound sense of personal failure that your flight is currently experiencing a small, yet impactful, operational delay."

A collective sigh of resignation swept through the QF437 crowd.

It was early, we were tired, and an 'operational delay' is aviation speak for 'we lost the pilot's keys.'

Penelope continued, her voice heavy with scripted empathy. "This is because of an unforeseen technical requirement involving a hydraulic gizmo and its connection to the overall structural integrity of the aircraft. We expect a new departure time in approximately one hour, but rest assured, we value your time and loyalty above all else."

Just as I settled in for an hour of doomscrolling, the loudspeaker crackled again. But this wasn't Penelope.

This voice was different: crisp, energetic, and possessed of a distinctly rural Australian cheer, the kind you get from someone who wakes up before the sun and enjoys it.

"G'day, everyone! This is Barry, your gate agent for Rex, Regional Express," the second voice chirped. Barry sounded like a man who ran marathons and drank only water with lemon. "And before we begin the boarding process for Rex Flight ZL660, the other Sydney service leaving from Gate 43, I just wanted to offer a quick, unsolicited, and highly relevant general update to the concourse."

He paused for dramatic effect.

The Qantas crowd, including myself, looked up, confused. Rex passengers at the next gate just grinned knowingly.

"We'd like to confirm for the record," Barry continued, his voice rising into a sing-song tone, "that Rex ZL660 is still operating perfectly on schedule. In fact, we're so on time, we might actually be five minutes early. We could theoretically push back now just to prove a point."

I heard Penelope gasp, a sound magnified horribly by the still-open Qantas microphone.

"And to address the mention of 'technical requirements' and 'hydraulic gizmos' from the other mob," Barry pressed on, sounding like he was suppressing laughter. "Rex would like to assure you that our planes use a robust, time-tested system known as 'having all the right bits attached before they leave the hangar.' It's a complex, proprietary process, but we manage it every day."

Penelope's voice squeaked back over the Qantas channel, cutting Barry off mid-sarcasm.

"Gate 43, this is Gate 42! Please be advised that you are broadcasting non-essential flight information onto a shared public frequency! Please refrain from unprofessional commentary!"

Barry's response was immediate and perfectly calibrated.

"Roger that, Penelope. Just sharing the good news! It's called transparency. Maybe if some people were more transparent, they wouldn't have unexpected technical requirements. Like how we're currently walking onto our plane, which is an action incompatible with sitting on the ground for an hour while someone tries to find a wrench."

He switched to his boarding voice, somehow even louder and more joyous. "Alright, ZL660 passengers! We are beginning priority boarding for all frequent flyers, and anyone who understands the concept of an airworthy timeline! Come on board; the coffee is hot, the seats don't have last week's biscotti crumbs, and we haven't needed a structural integrity check since we left the factory!"

A small, furious-looking man in a Qantas vest (presumably the pilot) stormed out of Gate 42's entry tunnel, gesticulating wildly toward Gate 43.

Penelope, visibly stressed, tried to salvage the situation.

"QF437 passengers, we are working diligently! And as a token of our heartfelt apology, we are pleased to offer you complimentary access to the Qantas App's premium content catalogue, including a selection of Australian sitcom reruns and a digital copy of our in-flight magazine, Qantas Traveller!"

Barry seized the moment.

"Rex ZL660, Zone B boarding! And just checking in on the Qantas Traveller offer—is that the issue? Did someone leave the hydraulic gizmo inside the magazine, and now they can't find the QR code? Tough break! We'll be viewing the real world from 30,000 feet, which is far more premium than any app catalogue."

He then adopted a dramatic whisper, still amplified to maximum volume. "They always panic-offer the magazine when the plane is broken."

Penelope's composure shattered.

"It is not broken! It is merely... optimising its pre-flight readiness! And we are now offering all QF437 passengers a choice of premium artisanal biscotti, flown in specifically from the finest wholesale bakery in Tullamarine! Please approach the desk one at a time!"

The Qantas crowd shuffled forward with the slow, defeated energy of people who knew artisanal biscotti could never fix a late flight.

Barry was relentless.

"Zone C boarding for ZL660! Just a heads-up, folks, if you see anyone queuing for what looks suspiciously like an expired digestive biscuit, that's not us. Our passengers are receiving complimentary on-time take-off and a view of the sunrise from cruising altitude, which is scientifically proven to be a better passenger experience than crunching on a stale oven tile!"

I was officially rooting for Barry. The sheer pettiness was magnificent. I was delayed, yes, but I was also being treated to the best airport theatre of my life.

The Rex boarding announcements continued, each zone a fresh layer of gloating.

"Final call for Rex ZL660! If you are still here, and you are not one of our confirmed, punctual customers, please observe the sight of an aircraft actually connecting its passengers with their intended destination. We call this 'Aviation in Action!' See you in Sydney, hopefully before lunchtime!"

Then, the pilot of QF437, that furious little man, marched back to the desk, grabbed the mic from Penelope, and bellowed, "We are Qantas! We are the Spirit of Australia! We will not be lectured by a company that runs its booking system off an old Commodore 64!"

Barry's voice, surprisingly calm, replied, "Sir, that Commodore 64 is on time."

The Qantas pilot dropped the mic and stormed off.

The loudspeaker system was silent for a moment.

The Rex gate was empty.

Their plane was visibly pulling away from the terminal.

The Qantas crowd stared at the empty space, with a mixture of annoyance and impressed bewilderment on their faces.

Penelope, completely deflated, picked up the microphone one last time.

"Right," she muttered, the sound heavy and defeated. "QF437 passengers. The artisanal biscotti are now double-sized. And... the hydraulic gizmo... it was fixed with a piece of duct tape and a firm word. We should board shortly."

With that, she turned and mumbled to herself: "I'm going to need a bigger coffee."

New Holland

"It just can't be that simple, Maura. It just can't. I know you are trying to teach me as much about Australia as possible, but I say it cannot be that simple."

I leaned back against the peeling vinyl of the pub booth, sipping my beer. I had just discovered a fun new historical fact, and my brain was refusing to process it reasonably.

Maura, who actually knows things, sighed into her cappuccino. "I just told you. The name Australia is derived from the Latin australis, meaning 'southern.' And specifically, it came from the hypothetical southern continent they used to draw on maps: Terra Australis, the 'Southern Land'."

"Southern Land," I interrupted, holding up a dramatic, wet finger.

"That's it? That's the entire creative process? We're talking about a country with marsupials, killer birds, and the world's most dangerous everything, and the best they could come up with was... direction?"

My mind immediately conjured an image of an ancient Roman committee meeting.

"Right, so we've found the big island. What should we call it?"

"Hmm. It's... south of here."

"Brilliant. Get the chisels. We'll call it 'South'."

"Think of the missed opportunities!" I pressed on.

"They could have called it 'Emu-Rage Island.' Or 'Oversized-Spider-Paradise.' Or, my personal favourite, 'The

Land of Upside-Down Weather.' But no. They went with 'Southern.' It's like naming your dog 'Dog'."

Maura gently tapped the table with her glass.

"You're forgetting the original name, which was arguably even less inspired. It was called New Holland for a long time, an English translation of the Dutch name. That name was first applied to the continent around 1643."

"New Holland!" I burst out laughing, momentarily forgetting my disappointment with the Latin.

"That sounds like a brand of industrial vacuum cleaner! 'Introducing the New Holland 5000: guaranteed to suck up all your unwanted Dutch settlements!' So, you're telling me that for over a century, the greatest island continent in the world was named after a slightly damp sock?"

"The Dutch were the first Europeans to sight much of the coastline," Maura explained, showing the patience of a saint dealing with an argumentative gnome. "They got the naming rights. It was just New Holland until the name Australia was popularised by the explorer Matthew Flinders around 1804."

I leaned forward conspiratorially. "Ah, Flinders. Now we have a villain. I bet he was a cartographer with absolutely zero imagination. I picture him standing on a beach in 1804, looking at a map that already says New Holland, and sighing."

"'Sir,' his assistant says, 'The king wants a new name. Something inspirational. Something that captures the vast, golden spirit of this frontier!'" I deepened my voice for Flinders. "'Inspirational, eh? Fine. Look, the map is still pointing south. Just write 'Australia.' I need to get back to my boat. The bilge water is getting too creative.'"

Maura chuckled, which was all the encouragement I needed.

"He actually was a serious and brilliant explorer who circumnavigated the continent. And he was the one who pushed for the name to reflect the ancient geographical idea of Terra Australis."

"Okay, fine, he was competent," I conceded grudgingly.

"But you have to admit, it sounds like he picked the name off a multiple-choice quiz. A. New Holland. B. Angry Kangaroo Land. C. Southern Land. He just circled C and said, 'Done. Where's my tea?'"

I paused, realizing the sheer bureaucratic weight of continent naming.

"But wait. If Flinders popularised it in 1804, why did they keep calling it New Holland in the official records?"

"It takes a while for government paperwork to catch up with popular usage, Leo. That's why it wasn't in official use until 1817," Maura replied, the exhaustion of explaining simple facts to me evident in her voice.

"Thirteen years!" I gasped, scandalised. "That's a full thirteen years of people sending letters to 'New Holland' only for them to arrive at the dead letter office because some desk jockey in London hadn't updated the colonial spreadsheet! They probably had to hold a four-day parliamentary debate on the correct Latin plural for 'Wallaby' before they could sign off on the name change in 1817."

I polished off the last of my fizzy lemonade.

"I still think my version, where an exhausted Matthew Flinders points south, yells 'Terra Australis is right there, mate, just call it Australia!' and then immediately takes a nap, is far superior. But I suppose a boring, technically correct history is also a history."

Maura just smiled, shaking her head. "It's a good thing you weren't in charge of naming things. We'd probably be living in 'The Big Dry Bit Where My Keys Always Fall Out of My Pocket'".

"It's catchy," I defended myself. "And at least it would be descriptive."

I Love Your Beautiful. Wait Let Me Finish

I, Leo Maxwell, aged seventeen, have always considered myself a poet of the modern age. A sensitive soul trapped in the body of a boy who trips over air and accidentally uses the word "moist" way too often.

But today was going to be different. Today, I was going to tell Maya how I felt.

Maya was the most spectacular person I had ever met. She could solve any math problem; her ponytail defied gravity, and she was the only person who understood the profound existential dread caused by running out of artisanal cheese crackers. We were sitting on the old picnic blanket under the enormous willow tree by the pond, the prime location for making life-altering declarations.

I had rehearsed this moment in the mirror for three days.

My plan was to start with a compliment so original, so surgically precise, that it would instantly convey the depth of my adoration. I didn't want to talk about her smile, her hair, or her kind heart. Anyone could see those. I wanted to compliment the feature that I found most scientifically and aesthetically compelling: her perfect, spherical organs of sight.

I had been spending a lot of time in biology class, and the geometry of the human form fascinated me. The human eye, protected by the orbital socket and cushioned by fat, is an engineering marvel. I watched them constantly, the way they tracked movement, the subtle way they seemed to bounce slightly when she laughed, catching the light like wet river stones.

This was it. This was my moment of poetic genius.

I took a deep breath, the scent of damp grass and existential anxiety filling my lungs. Maya was meticulously sorting her gummy bears by colour, a ritual I found incredibly charming.

"Maya," I started, my voice cracking slightly, which was a nice touch, I thought. Very dramatic.

She looked up, a purple gummy bear poised mid-air. "Yeah, Leo?"

I leaned in, deciding to ditch the intro and go straight for the killer line. I tried to mentally combine 'perfectly round,' 'glistening,' and 'full of life' into one powerful image, but my brain, a known traitor, used the most juvenile synonyms it could find.

I whispered, with all the intensity of a young man committing to a terrible mistake: "I love your round, bouncy, and beautiful balls."

The purple gummy bear missed her mouth entirely, landing with a soft, sticky thwack on her knee.

The silence that followed wasn't just quiet; it was the kind of silence that demands its own soundtrack, preferably one featuring a needle scratching off a record. Maya didn't blush. She didn't giggle. She just stared at me, her actual intended-target eyeballs narrowed into slits of cold judgment.

She slowly wiped the purple gummy bear off her jeans. "You're so cheap!" she said, her voice dangerously flat. She was insulted, but not for the reason I thought. "Is that all you love in me?"

Oh no. She thinks I'm superficial!

My poetic masterpiece had backfired. She thought I was reducing her entire magnificent being to one physical characteristic. I needed to pivot immediately and prove that my appreciation was deep, not shallow. I needed to detail the secondary features of the spherical objects in question. I needed to mention the iris and the pupil. I shook my head violently, scrambling to correct my error.

"No! No, no, no," I insisted, grabbing her wrist impulsively.

"You don't understand! I'm talking about the details! The mesmerizing depth!"

I pointed a trembling finger toward her face, aiming for her eye but missing, pointing instead somewhere near her ear.

"No; I love those dark circles in the middle too. I can keep looking at them for long."

Wait, 'dark circles'? That makes it sound as if she's tired. Or a panda. I immediately regretted the word choice, but it was too late. The damage had been done.

Maya snatched her hand back as if I'd tried to stick her with a cactus.

The flat, cold anger had been replaced by a fiery, righteous indignation that made my stomach drop into my runners. This time, she didn't sound insulted; she sounded genuinely furious and done.

"This is enough! I'm done with you!" she yelled, pushing herself off the blanket and onto her feet, ready to bolt.

Panic, cold and sharp, finally cut through my internal monologue about synonyms. She thinks I'm a complete, absolute creep! She thinks I'm talking about... something else! The word 'balls' combined with 'dark circles in the middle' had created an unholy, completely unintended description.

"No, wait, Maya!" I scrambled to stand up, knocking over the basket of half-eaten sandwiches. The bread rolls, which were also round, went rolling down the small incline toward the creek. "You have to let me finish!"

She stood rigid, arms crossed, tapping her foot with the impatience of a highly intelligent girl whose favourite hobby was now ending me.

"I meant your round, bouncy, beautiful eyeballs with the dark irises in the middle!" I pleaded, emphasizing the key anatomical terms. "The sclera is white, and the pupil lets in the light! They're fantastic! I meant I love the way you see the world!"

She paused, her expression cycling through confusion, horror, and finally, a deep, crushing wave of exhaustion.

She stared at me for three long seconds.

Maya then raised her hand slowly, bringing it up to cover her entire face. She didn't move or speak for several heartbeats.

"FACEPALM!"

I watched her walk away, shoulders hunched, disappearing behind the jacaranda tree. I was left alone on the picnic blanket, surrounded by gummy bears and a trio of escaped, rolling bread rolls, which were now gently bobbing in the creek.

I stared at the water, contemplating the fact that I had just ruined my entire future over a poorly phrased compliment regarding the structural integrity of her ocular globes. I sighed, slumping back onto the blanket. I really should have just complimented her ponytail. It was much easier to describe without sounding like a rejected villain from a creepy children's cartoon.

I suddenly realised that the reason her actual eyeballs looked so bouncy was that she had been vigorously shaking her head the entire time I was talking.

That realisation was almost worse than the initial misunderstanding.

Piloerection

I've been cursed. Not with vampirism or the ability to communicate with houseplants, but with something far more embarrassing: involuntary piloerection.

Most people get goosebumps for profound reasons.

A breathtaking performance of "Nessun Dorma," a sudden chill, or perhaps seeing a puppy successfully navigate a tiny staircase.

My skin?

My skin responds to the existential dread of Monday.

Or, worse, to the sheer, soul-crushing neutrality of a mid-morning utility bill.

I first realised the depth of my affliction last Tuesday.

I was in a quarterly budget meeting. Mr Henderson, a man whose voice could put a glass of milk to sleep, was droning on about "leveraging synergies across Q4." I was barely listening, just trying to keep my eyelids from fusing shut, when I felt it: a ripple of biological horror spreading up my arms.

My shirt sleeves were rolled up.

The hairs on my forearms were suddenly ramrod straight, like a tiny forest of surprised exclamation points.

Why, body? I mentally screamed.

Is this it?

Is this the moment of profound corporate truth?

Has "synergy" finally transcended language and achieved a state of pure, terrifying power?

I glanced around, panicked.

Did anyone see my arm hair trying to signal Morse code?

Thankfully, everyone was as glazed over as I was.

I subtly slid my hands under the table, praying for the sensation to pass.

It didn't.

It only intensified when Mr Henderson switched from discussing spreadsheets to discussing the correct way to load a dishwasher.

I spend my life in a constant state of defensive arousal.

I don't need a roller coaster to get my heart pounding; I just need to open my bank statement. My body believes every minor inconvenience is a surprise encounter with a territorial Big Red in the bush.

The other day, I was at Woolies, waiting in line behind a woman purchasing exactly thirty-seven cans of tuna. The cashier, a charming young man named Kyle, was scanning them with the speed of an Olympic snail.

Suddenly, the music system played "Smooth Operator" by Sade.

Now, Sade is great, but she is the auditory equivalent of a velvet bathmat.

There is nothing shocking, cold, or inspiring about her music.

Yet there it was: a full-body, shiver-inducing eruption.

My shoulders seized up.

My neck hairs stood at attention like tiny, uniformed sentinels.

I looked like I was having a mild, erotic seizure induced by light jazz.

Kyle looked up. "Rough day, mate?" he asked, pointing to my chest.

My nipple-hairs were apparently attempting to tunnel out of my shirt.

I cleared my throat. "Just the texture of the tuna cans," I lied, scraping my voice up from the deepest part of my throat.

"It's overwhelming. So metallic. So cylindrical. It's a lot to process."

He just nodded slowly, probably earmarking me as the tuna-obsessed weirdo.

My piloerection is a betrayal.

It makes my outward appearance lie about my inner state.

I could be thinking, I really need to change the lint filter in the washing machine soon, and my skin will react as if I have just witnessed a miracle.

I'm thinking it's a commentary on modern life.

Maybe my nervous system is just tired of pretending to be calm and collected. Maybe the hair on my arms is just screaming what I can't: "I am not okay with this! This level of administrative paperwork/mildly retro music/lukewarm coffee is unacceptable to the ancestral human in me!"

Now, if you'll excuse me, I need to go refill the office printer paper. I'm bracing myself for the emotional whiplash, because I'm pretty sure the clean, white edge of the new ream is going to give me chills.

The Blind Leading the Blind and the Bank Consultant

I exist primarily to justify my own fees. I'm a high-value, cross-jurisdictional financial restructuring consultant, which is corporate shorthand for "the guy who flies Sydney to Perth at 5:00 AM on a Tuesday to tell mid-level management they've been using too many Post-it notes."

I live by data, logic, and a pathological need for efficiency.

This particular Tuesday was already a statistical anomaly of misery.

I was wedged into seat 27B, a window seat I'd only taken because 27A, the aisle, was already occupied by a man who looked like he'd been medically fused with his laptop bag.

My entire personal ecosystem, the quarterly projections, the three-month EBITDA forecast, and my artisanal almond croissant, was currently under threat from the sheer proximity of other human beings.

We had taxied out, lumbered toward the runway, and were just starting that terrifying internal calculation—Will this metal bird defy gravity today?—when the engines whined down to an embarrassed cough.

The cabin lights flickered, and a sound came over the intercom that always precedes bad news: the clack of a microphone being cleared by someone who definitely does not want to clear a microphone.

"Ladies and gentlemen," a voice, marginally less confident than a puppy facing a staircase, chirped. "This is Captain Miller speaking. We appear to have a minor technical anomaly with the starboard wing's hydraulics. Nothing to worry about, naturally, but the engineers need to take a quick look. We'll be heading back to the gate, and for safety, the ground crew has requested that all passengers deplane and wait in the terminal."

An audible groan rolled through the cabin, a collective, visceral reaction from people whose timelines were now being subjected to the cruel, arbitrary chaos of thermodynamics.

I, however, instantly sprang into action. Not in panic, but in pure, clinical efficiency. I calculated the opportunity cost of this delay: 45 minutes of work lost versus 90 minutes of potential work time gained if I could find a quiet corner with power sockets near the gate. It was statistically a wash, but the principle remained: move fast.

I stood, grabbed my meticulously labelled briefcase, and joined the flow of grumpy, sighing humanity shuffling back up the aisle with me holding up the rear. We were about halfway to the front door when I noticed him.

He was sitting calmly in the first row of economy, 10A, a distinguished gentleman in his sixties. Beside him, tucked neatly into the footwell, was a magnificent Golden Retriever, its harness glinting faintly in the cabin light.

The man was blind, and the dog was his eyes.

As every other person ahead of me and across the aisle stood up to deplane, this man remained perfectly still. The dog remained perfectly still. They were an island of serenity in a river of middle-management angst.

My consultant brain, which rarely encounters a problem it can't bill an hourly rate to solve, briefly short-circuited. Protocol failure. How does he get off the plane?

I paused, half-raised my hand, and was about to offer assistance—a noble, non-billable act that would surely put me 0.5% ahead on my Karma metric for the quarter when a new figure strode into the frame.

It was Captain Miller.

He wasn't wearing his captain's hat. He was wearing his captain's aura, which is more intimidating. He stopped beside the blind gentleman, knelt down with unexpected grace, and whispered.

"Sir, apologies for the inconvenience. We're going to get you back to the terminal. I've got this."

The gentleman nodded, offered a gentle pat to his dog, and smoothly passed the leash to the captain.

This is where the laws of corporate travel physics officially broke down.

The Captain stood up, adjusted the leash in his grip, and then, in a movement so sudden and theatrical it might have been choreographed, he pulled a pair of mirrored, dark sunglasses from his breast pocket and smoothly slid them onto the bridge of his nose.

The effect was instantaneous and baffling.

Captain Miller, the man who was supposed to be in command of approximately eighty-three tonnes of flying metal and the lives contained within it, was now wearing pitch-black, impenetrable aviator sunglasses, indoors, and holding the leash of a guide dog.

He gave a sharp tug on the leash and said, "Alright, let's go, buddy."

Then, Captain Miller, guided by a highly trained Golden Retriever, began his smooth, confident walk down the jetway and into the brightly lit terminal building.

A flight attendant, bless her cotton socks, was walking about six paces behind them, her face a mask of professionally suppressed horror, holding up her hand to help the elderly gentleman.

The moment this surreal tableau—the Captain in Dark Sunglasses, led by a Seeing-Eye Dog, followed by a Mortified Flight Attendant and Blind Passenger —passed through the narrow glass tunnel of the jetway, the collective consciousness of the deplaning passengers shattered.

I heard a sound somewhere between a gasp and a strangled pterodactyl cry. Then, the whispered, panicked assessments began.

"Did you see that?!"

"The pilot is blind!"

"He just walked off the plane! The Captain! He's blind!"

"The hydraulic anomaly wasn't the problem; he was the problem!"

The calculated, efficient flow of humanity immediately reversed.

People, marketing managers, organisation coordinators, even the laptop-bag man, stopped dead. Instead of heading to the terminal lounge, they scrambled backward, shoving each other to retrieve their carry-on bags from the overhead compartments.

The rush hour became the stampede hour.

I watched in stunned silence as dozens of highly paid, highly educated professionals made the immediate, catastrophic logical leap that the Captain of their flight had just intentionally revealed that he possessed zero operational visibility.

They didn't consider that maybe, just maybe, he was helping a passenger, and the sunglasses were a hilarious mistake or a corporate uniform accessory.

No.

The evidence was irrefutable: the pilot needed the dog. The flight was structurally compromised.

Within three minutes, the entire cabin was empty, save for me. The other passengers were already halfway to the service desks, frantically rebooking themselves onto any competitor flight that wasn't piloted by a visually impaired, sunglass-wearing dog walker.

I stood there, surrounded by the detritus of hasty abandonment: half-eaten newspapers, discarded boarding passes, and the faint, sweet scent of panic sweat. I looked around. 27B, the last seat in my dreary section. And then I heard the click of a heel.

The flight attendant, the one who had followed the captain's farcical procession, reappeared. She was massaging her temples.

"Sir, are you the only one left?" She said, her voice strained.

I nodded slowly, adjusting my cufflinks, and answered: "It would appear so."

She sighed, a sound of utter defeat.

"The gentleman needed a hand. Captain Miller thought he was being funny. He always wears those ridiculous sunglasses. Anyway, the engineers just finished the repair. We're ready to go."

She paused, looked at the empty plane, and then a mischievous glint returned to her eyes. "Well, Mr Peterson. Since you are our only remaining passenger, and we can't fly a near-empty plane, we're consolidating. Follow me, please."

I was ushered through the curtain, past the gloriously empty galley, and into the sacred space of First Class. I sank into a leather throne; a glass of 2008 Barossa Shiraz appeared in my hand, and the scent of expensive quiet filled my nostrils.

I watched the Sydney skyline shrink, a solitary figure in a cavernous, opulent cabin. The lesson I realised was not about hydraulics or even about efficiency. The true, billable-hour lesson of this trip was this: sometimes, the greatest professional advantage you can gain is simply by not being the one who makes the immediate, most emotionally reactive assumption.

Also, never interrupt a captain who's attempting absurdist comedy. You might just get an upgrade out of it, and for the record, 2/B never smelled so good as it did when it was thirty-thousand feet below me.

I closed my eyes and decided that, for today only, the quarterly projections could wait until I landed. The cost of a few hours of billable time was definitely justified by the pure, undiluted joy of this leather-bound silence.

Flickering

I slumped deeper into my recliner, the remote control in my hand. Pushing the buttons, I flickered through an endless parade of channels: Netflix, Amazon Prime Video, Hulu, Disney+, HBO Max, Peacock, YouTube TV, and Paramount+ and many more. Nothing to watch.

Twenty-five years.

Twenty-five years of this ritual, this nightly quest for something, anything remotely watchable.

Suddenly, a scent drifted into the living room.

Something warm and subtly floral, like lavender and a hint of something sweet, perhaps the vanilla candle she'd lit earlier. Then, she appeared in front of me, drying her hands on a tea towel, a stray wisp of hair covering a little of her beautiful face, Agatha.

She wasn't wearing anything special.

Just her old, faded blue dressing gown, the one with the slightly frayed cuff. Her glasses were perched on her head.

She yawned, did a small, elegant stretch, and then her eyes, those familiar, kind eyes, met mine.

And in that moment, as the remote slipped from my grasp and clattered softly to the rug, I saw her.

Not the woman who nagged me about leaving my socks on the floor, or the one who insisted on watching those terrible period dramas. I saw the girl I'd fallen in love with, the vibrant, witty, beautiful woman who had chosen me, flaws, and all, for a quarter of a century. The way the soft lamplight caught the silver threads in her hair, making them gleam like moonlight.

Agatha smiled and asked: "Find anything good?"

A wave of profound, overwhelming affection washed over me. She was simply breathtaking.

After all these years, the mundane had melted away, revealing the extraordinary. I felt a lump in my throat, a sudden urge to tell her everything, to wrap her in my arms and remind her how truly cherished she was. How much I wanted to take her to bed and make love to her.

I cleared my throat, a heartfelt declaration forming on my lips. "Agatha," I began, my voice thick with emotion, "you know, after all this time, you are still the most..."

Then, suddenly, a crushing wave of exhaustion hit me.

My eyelids felt heavy; my muscles ached from a long day.

The thought of getting up, of engaging in anything more strenuous than changing the channel, felt utterly insurmountable.

I just wanted to close my eyes.

"...comfortable person I know," I finished, stifling a yawn. "And frankly, I'm too tired to move. Can you grab the remote? I think I just changed it to the shopping channel."

"Sure," was all she said as she sat in her own recliner and started flicking through channels once again.

Goodbyes

Arthur lived in the quiet, salt-sprayed solitude of a small Western Australian town, a widower for five years, running a hardware store that had belonged to his father. Eleanor lived near Sydney, surrounded by the constant, soft dampness of the ocean. A widow for six years, tending a small but successful organic flower farm. They were literally separated by the width of a continent, almost four thousand kilometres and three time zones; the distance being the single, defining boundary of their blossoming, impossible romance.

They had met, as so many modern hearts do, in the gentle, anonymous refuge of an online forum dedicated to classic literature and quiet grief. Arthur had posted about the difficulty of reading Jane Austen now that the comfortable, shared silence of his marriage was gone. Eleanor had replied, comparing the experience in trying to listen to a waltz alone. They began exchanging emails, then long, rambling voice notes, and finally, daily video calls that transcended the simple limitations of geography.

Their connection was rooted not in the giddy, demanding excitement of new love, but in the profound, sympathetic recognition of shared loss. They didn't need to explain the sudden, startling emptiness in the kitchen, or the guilt that clung to moments of unexpected joy. They spoke the same language of bereavement. Arthur could tell Eleanor about the way the light fell differently on his wife's favourite armchair, and Eleanor could confess to Arthur how she still talked to her late husband while pruning roses, and neither would feel the need to offer hollow reassurance.

Their relationship was built on acceptance—acceptance of the past, acceptance of their current solitude, and, most crucially, acceptance of the barrier that fate had erected between them. Arthur had commitments: an old, sprawling farmhouse he couldn't leave, a dependent, aging sister, and a small-town economy that relied on him. Eleanor had responsibilities woven into the damp soil of her life: grandchildren she saw daily, a thriving business built with her own hands, and a deep-seated reluctance to surrender the last physical geography her husband had known. They were not free to move, and they both knew it. One evening, Arthur watched the clock tick past midnight, the west coast wind howling faintly outside his window, as Eleanor, three hours behind him, showed him the first bloom of a rare Japanese clematis on her farm. Her voice, tired and soft, was full of quiet pride.

"It's beautiful, El," he murmured. "I wish I could see it in daylight. Feel that breeze on my face, too."

Eleanor paused, her face clouding only momentarily. "I wish you could, too, Art. But you know what we have, don't you? It's not the sight or the feel, it's the knowing. I know that when you're watching the sunrise on the other coast, and you know I just saw the moon set over me."

That was the essence of their solace: a love that was a shared, immense sky, not a confined hearth. It was a beautiful, non-physical companionship that asked nothing of them except their truth. Their intimacy was purely conversational, distilled, and potent. They exchanged books, reading chapters over the phone, sometimes falling asleep with the line still open, waking to the sound of quiet breathing thousands of miles away. It was a love that couldn't be tarnished by the mundanity of shared chores or the friction of physical proximity. It was perfect because it was geographically impossible.

The hardest part was the conscious decision, made without formal declaration, to never close the distance. They occasionally spoke of visiting, but the planning always stalled, inevitably derailed by an honest question: What would be the point? A week together would only make the return to separation unbearable. They cherished the stability of their remote affection more than the fleeting, sharp pleasure of a temporary meeting.

"If you came here," Eleanor once said, her voice steady, "we'd have to say goodbye at the airport. That goodbye would be real. What we have now, this... this cannot say goodbye."

Arthur understood. He was healed by her presence in his headphones, not by the promise of her touch. He knew his responsibility to his town, and she to her farm. Their bond was a lighthouse beam—a constant, steady, necessary light that guided them through their individual darknesses. It was not a harbour, for they were both irrevocably moored to their old lives, but it was the sure knowledge that another light was always there, shining back. And so, they continued. Arthur still woke before dawn in Maine; Eleanor still stayed up late in Oregon. They were two silent stars, orbiting separate poles, but forever linked by the gentle gravity of their chosen, accepted distance, finding in their impossible love a profound and lasting peace.

The Day My World Spun

I still remember the day I found you;
My entire world began to revolve around you.
I spoke a simple wish: Will you be mine?

Now you reside in a peace beyond this world.
Yet, if I could hold on to you now,
To cling to you now and forever, I would.

Will our paths cross again, my love?
Can we finally share a love made whole?
Because without your light, I cannot live.

You left me, darling, and the solitude is endless.
Please send a sign; tell me you loved me solely.
And that the heart you gave me will always, forever, be
mine.

The next time our souls meet,
I promise I will find you, my sweet love.
What is life if not this determined search?

I speak it again, my heart's refrain:
Tell me your love for me is the only truth.
So, this silence is not forever lonely.
And that you'll always, truly, be mine.

Debriefing Log 47-E:
Terra: TERRA

I adjusted the pressure seals on my cranial hood and cycled the air in the Debriefing Module, letting the sterile, recycled atmosphere of the Aetherium chase away the lingering, discordant scent of the third planet. Terra. Earth.

Across the polished obsidian table, Zorp, our chief field operative, was already settled. Zorp's method is aggressive; his data collection is relentless. My own, Xylar, is linguistic and psychological. We are rarely in agreement on the root cause of Terran irrationality, but on one point, we were perfectly aligned: the planet's food nomenclature was a Class 9 cognitive hazard.

"Report log 47-E initiated," I stated, the synthesised tenor of my voice echoing slightly in the module. "Subject: Culinary Linguistics and Semantic Deception. Operative Zorp, are you prepared to compare data?"

Zorp's primary optic flickered—the Terran equivalent of a heavy sigh. "I am prepared, Xylar, though my entire digestive tract is still attempting to process the ontological horror of what they call 'food.' Let's begin with the initial list of linguistic tripwires you flagged for analysis. Specifically, the regional anomalies."

"Anomalies, Zorp, or deliberate, systemic deception? That is the crux of the matter," I countered, pulling up my first data slate. The image projected onto the table was of a viscous, orange-amber condiment.

"We begin with Duck Sauce," I announced, gesturing to the image. "During my observation of the Chinese American preparation complex—a fascinating cultural hybrid, but I digress—I was consistently presented with this item alongside fried dough parcels. My linguistic processors immediately prioritised the 'Duck' component. Given the prevalence of Anas platyrhynchos in their diet, I assumed this was a reduction or essence of the avian's tissue, perhaps a clarified bone stock or a highly concentrated fatty emulsion."

Zorp made a low-frequency hum of agreement. "My sensory data matched. The name implies a primary ingredient of duck. Upon testing, the sauce was revealed to be a sugary concoction, primarily fruit pulp—apricots, plums, or peaches—sweetened with glucose derivatives and vinegar."

I steepled my multi-jointed fingers. "Precisely. The total duck content, Zorp, across all 1,137 samples recorded in Sector 14, was precisely zero. Not a molecule. It is a complete misnomer. They assign the name of an animal to a simple fruit preserve purely for context—it is served with duck, so they call it Duck Sauce. It is an associative lie. This is not semantic evolution; it is linguistic sloppiness. Why call it 'Plum or Apricot Dipping Preserve' when they can simply lie about the animal content?"

Zorp tapped the table. "It generates an anticipatory signal that is incorrect. The Earthling mind accepts this contradiction. It sets a precedent for all subsequent linguistic anomalies. It is a trap built of laziness, or perhaps, a primitive form of humour rooted in disappointment. If the first thing is a lie, why would they be truthful about the next?"

"A perfect transition to geographical confusion," I said, scrolling to the next item.

"Next, we examine the geographical component. I flag for your analysis the English muffin." The image of the pale, porous, flat bread-like disc appeared.

"This one was less disturbing than the Duck Sauce, but equally confusing," Zorp noted. "It is a simple, yeast-leavened bread product. Why is it 'English'? My research traced its origin to the late 19th-century of the North American continent, specifically the area known as New York City. The word 'muffin' itself is of ambiguous, ancient European origin, but the product, as consumed, is demonstrably North American."

"It is a marketing lie, Zorp," I deduced. "They attach a foreign modifier—'English'—to imply an old-world authenticity or quality that the product does not inherently possess. It serves no descriptive function. It is not only or even primarily consumed by the English. It is a manufactured cultural borrowing, a linguistic passport fraud."

I paused for effect, then projected the next item: German Chocolate Cake. "This is worse. It is a multi-layered cake product comprising specific ingredients—custard, pecans, and coconut—that define the dish. The name implies a German origin, a national descriptor that should anchor its history and tradition."

Zorp bristled. "My archives show this product originated in the 1950s in the state of Texas, North America. It was named after an individual, Sam German, who developed a type of dark baking chocolate for the Baker's brand. The chocolate was simply a component, yet the final cake product appropriated the modifier 'German' from the creator's surname, thus implying a false national origin. It is a genealogical lie disguised as a culinary descriptor."

"Exactly," I sighed, mapping the trajectory of Terran deception. "Duck Sauce lies about the content. English muffins lie about the culture. German Chocolate Cake lies about the lineage. There is no predictive utility in their language. It misleads the consumer, forcing them into a state of perpetual epistemological uncertainty about their meal."

I mentioned the next dish. The image showed a thick, golden sauce poured over toasted bread. "This, Zorp, caused a significant spike in my empathy circuits. Welsh Rabbit."

Zorp leaned forward, his primary optic widening. "The name suggests a simple, pastoral dish—perhaps rabbit stewed in a unique manner attributed to the region of Wales. Given the history of hunting on this planet, it was plausible. I prepared for data assimilation of Lagomorpha tissue."

"And what did you find?" I prompted.

"Zero Lagomorpha tissue. None," Zorp confirmed, his voice registering a low-level disturbance. "It is melted cheese and beer poured over toasted bread. The name is completely unconnected to its ingredients. The linguistic implication of consuming a small, furry, indigenous animal is entirely gratuitous."

"The original term, Zorp, was likely 'Welsh Rarebit'—a term that seems to derive from 'rare bit,' a piece of a delicacy. It was corrupted, likely by mockery, to 'Rabbit'—suggesting that the poor inhabitants of Wales, lacking the means for actual rabbit, were forced to eat cheese as a substitute. The phrase is a historical insult, a regional slur perpetuated for centuries in the guise of a dish."

"A dish that lies about its primary protein and simultaneously insults the people whose name it has borrowed," Zorp muttered, adjusting his hood. "They encode their cruelty and their historical biases directly into their culinary naming. It is a recursive linguistic attack."

I nodded slowly. "It proves that Terran nomenclature is a system of psychological warfare against the consumer, designed to make every meal a test of faith."

I hesitated before projecting the next image. This required a content warning, even for us. "We move now to the anatomical category. I present to you: Rocky Mountain Oysters."

The image showed several deep-fried, irregularly shaped objects coated in a seasoned batter.

Zorp emitted a sharp burst of static—an involuntary neurological defence mechanism. "The sensory data on this was... confusing. The name suggests bivalve molluscs harvested from the Rocky Mountain region. The geological name is correct. The animal's name is a profound fabrication. I ran DNA analysis."

"And the result?"

"The result, Xylar, is that they are excised male reproductive organs—testicular tissue—from either bovine or porcine life forms. The term 'Oysters' is a deliberate, sickening euphemism designed to conceal the true biological nature of the dish. They are not molluscs. They are gonads. They are testicles." Zorp repeated the word with clinical revulsion.

"The horror, Zorp, is not just the content but the intent," I said, my processors whirring to articulate the depth of the deception. "They know the true name is unpalatable to most. Therefore, they deliberately choose the name of an expensive, desirable, unrelated seafood item to trick or cajole the diner. It transforms a simple act of consumption into an act of covert biological transgression."

"Why not simply call them 'Fried Bull Testicles'?" Zorp demanded. "It is descriptively accurate."

"Because they understand the power of linguistic camouflage," I explained. "By attaching a luxury term ('Oysters') to a waste product ('Testicles'), they can market the unthinkable. It is a linguistic act of alchemy, turning biological residue into a regional delicacy. The Earthling mind is constantly performing this kind of semantic negotiation with reality."

I quickly moved on, needing to cleanse the palate of that last item. "Let us try another animal-based lie, this time less anatomically invasive: Bombay Duck." The image was of a long, thin, silver-coloured, dried fish.

Zorp groaned, a sound like grinding tectonic plates. "Another avian lie! When I encountered this in a South Asian cuisine preparation unit, my initial data query returned a negative on duck content, but positive on fish. It is a small lizardfish, Harpadon nehereus, which is dried and salted."

"The question is the appellation," I pressed. "Why 'Duck'?"

"Theories are convoluted," Zorp reported. "One suggests that during the era of British colonial administration, the fish was transported on mail trains labelled 'Bombay Dawk'—'Dawk' meaning 'mail' or 'post' in a local dialect. Non-native speakers phonetically corrupted the term into 'Duck.' So, it is a lie of translation, a mistake born of linguistic laziness, which was then permanently codified into the food's name. A phonetic corruption of a foreign word, combined with a geographical identifier, resulting in the name of an unrelated animal."

"So, to summarise," I said, mapping the chain of failure. "It is a fish named 'Duck,' which got its name from a misheard word for 'Mail,' which was itself transported from the city of 'Bombay.' Four layers of semantic noise for a piece of dried fish. It is not designed to convey information; it conveys the history of human error and colonization."

The meeting was taking a toll. I could see Zorp was activating his low-level stabilisation field.

"Let us examine the last pair of animal misnomers, starting with the bizarre recreational product known as Puppy Chow," I said, showing an image of a mixture of cereal pieces, peanut butter, chocolate, and powdered sugar.

"This one gave me a diagnostic panic," Zorp confessed. "Puppy Chow is, descriptively, food for a young canine. The product is named identically to the biological necessity of a young mammal. Yet this Puppy Chow is a highly addictive, hyper-caloric sweet snack consumed primarily by adult humans. The name is a bizarre appropriation of pet-food nomenclature."

"It's a linguistic wink, Zorp," I theorised. "A reference to the snack's addictive, almost compulsive nature, suggesting one might 'devour' it like an unrefined animal. It's an act of self-deprecating humour and marketing, leveraging the familiarity of a common pet food product to sell a children's dessert. They will equate their own snack consumption to that of a domesticated mammal, a stunning lack of self-respect."

I quickly transitioned to the counterpoint: sweetbreads. The image was of a piece of pale, firm, cooked offal.

"Here, we have another anatomical euphemism, but one rooted in antiquity," I began. "Sweetbreads. The word 'sweet' suggests a desirable flavour, and 'bread' suggests a simple, starchy carbohydrate."

"And it is glandular tissue," Zorp finished, cutting me off. "The thymus or the pancreas of a calf or lamb. The 'sweet' descriptor is historically dubious, perhaps only 'sweet' when compared to other, more pungent offal. The 'bread' descriptor is entirely erroneous, possibly a corruption of the Old English word 'bræd,' meaning 'flesh' or 'roast.' It is a double-layered lie across multiple millennia."

"It's a linguistic fossil, Zorp," I clarified. "A name so old that its parts no longer mean what they should mean, yet they keep it because of tradition. They are eating a biological organ under the cover of a pleasingly named, starchy baked good. The cognitive dissonance is staggering. They knowingly perpetuate ancient lies to make the unpalatable palatable."

"We have two last items, both concerning preparation and national attribution," I said. "First, the Scotch Egg." The image was of a hard-boiled egg wrapped in sausage meat, coated in breadcrumbs, and deep-fried.

Zorp tapped his optic thoughtfully. "The name implies an egg from Scotland. But the dish is merely an egg that has been prepared in a certain manner, possibly originating in London or maybe North Africa. The 'Scotch' is another geographic marker applied arbitrarily, much like the 'English' muffin, a lie of national origin."

"But look at the linguistic simplicity," I pointed out. "'Scotch Egg.' It is purely descriptive in its parts yet entirely misleading in its whole. It should be called a 'Sausage-Encased, Breaded, Deep-Fried Hard-Boiled Egg.' But they truncate it. They select the least-descriptive, most-arbitrary modifier ('Scotch') and fuse it to the most prominent ingredient ('Egg'). It is a minimalist lie."

"It is the culmination of all the previous errors: geographic falsehood, oversimplification, and marketing convenience," Zorp observed.

I saved the last item for the inevitable philosophical breakdown. "Finally, Zorp, we come to French Toast." The image was thick slices of bread, soaked in an egg/milk mixture and fried until soft and custard-like.

"The most baffling, perhaps, because of the internal contradiction of the descriptor," Zorp stated. "Toast, by its very definition, is bread subjected to heat until it becomes dry, firm, and brittle. The preparation known as French Toast—and historical evidence suggests it has pre-French origins, of course—involves soaking the bread until it is wet, soft, and custard-like. The name is an anti-descriptor. It is the antonym of the state of the bread. It is anti-toast."

"And yet, they call it Toast," I whispered, allowing the absurdity of the statement to hang in the sterile air. "Why? Because it was once, briefly, toasted bread? Because the word 'Toast' is the most familiar denominator? It is a monument to their willingness to live with a constant, obvious falsehood in their everyday lives."

I deactivated the visual display and leaned back; the analysis was complete. The module was quiet except for the hum of the recycler.

"So, Zorp, we have analysed ten items," I summarised. "The data is consistent: Terran culinary nomenclature is not designed for clarity, logic, or accurate description. It is a labyrinth of semantic traps, historical accidents, and deliberate misdirection."

Duck Sauce, Bombay Duck, Welsh Rabbit: Animal-based lies designed to mislead about protein content.

English Muffin, German Chocolate Cake, Scotch Egg, French Toast: geographic or preparation lies designed to fabricate origin or contradict the final state.

Rocky Mountain Oysters, Sweetbreads: Anatomical lies designed to euphemize the consumption of undesirable organs.

Puppy Chow: a marketing lie designed to equate human consumption with animal behaviour.

"The conclusion, Xylar, must be that their cognitive function is profoundly compromised," Zorp stated firmly. "They tolerate—even celebrate—this level of systematic falsehood. They navigate their planet under a constant barrage of semantic contradictions, and it does not impede their ability to function. In fact, it seems to enhance their commercial engine. Why must they lie about a fruit preserve by calling it Duck Sauce, or lie about testicles by calling them Oysters?"

"Because they are masters of cognitive framing, Zorp," I explained. "They are not looking for truth in the name; they are looking for a story. The lie becomes a tradition. By calling it 'Duck Sauce,' they create a contextual link to an entire meal. By calling them 'Rocky Mountain Oysters,' they transform an act of culinary frugality into a daring, regionally specific experience. The names are not definitions; they are marketing campaigns that have survived for decades, even centuries."

"They value linguistic excitement over accuracy," Zorp concluded, his voice low with disappointment. "They prefer the charming deceit of a 'Welsh Rabbit'—a cheese dish named after a lie about a missing animal—to the boring truth. This shows a high tolerance for manufactured reality. It is a survival trait, perhaps, allowing them to ignore the vast existential contradictions of their own species by focusing on the small, manageable culinary contradictions."

"Indeed. Their entire language is an onion of ambiguity," I agreed. "We must append this finding to the final report. Terra is a planet that names its fried gonads after bivalves and its fruit sauces after ducks. We must recommend a Level Five quarantine on all direct linguistic contact until their naming conventions achieve a minimum level of predictive utility, or until we can understand why they enjoy confusing themselves so much."

Zorp stood up, his posture rigid. "Agreed. I am already compiling a secondary list, Xylar. We must next analyse 'Red Velvet Cake'—it is neither red nor velvet—and 'Head

Cheese'—which is neither head nor cheese. The task is unending."

I sighed; the recycled air suddenly felt very heavy.

"The things we do for Xenolinguistics. End report log 47-E."

Cleansed by the Downpour

As I pushed open the front door, a cool, clean scent wafted in, signalling a shift in the morning's mood. The sky was a soft, uniform grey, and the air held a unique stillness just before a good downpour. My usual morning walk is a predictable routine, a chance to clear my head, but today promised something different. There was a faint, almost imperceptible hum in the atmosphere, a quiet prelude.

Then, the first drops arrived.

They weren't aggressive, just a scattering of cool pinpricks on my exposed skin. I felt them land on my forehead, a surprising chill on my nose, and then trace faint lines down my cheeks.

Each drop was incredibly light yet carried an undeniable coolness that made me shiver slightly, in a good way. I paused for a moment, closing my eyes, letting the initial soft drumming play out on my jacket and hair.

The rain picked up — a steady patter that quickly increased.

This rain did not send me scrambling for cover.

No, this was a steady, refreshing shower, almost playful, as if the sky itself were having a brisk wash.

It ran through my greyish hair, wetting it instantly and soaking me totally. I felt with each drop, as if the world around me seemed to awaken. The sound of the raindrops hitting the leaves, the footpath, the distant rumble on rooftops—it all blended into a soothing, natural symphony.

The noise of the rain created a kind of serene bubble, muffling the usual urban car sounds as they drove by and allowing my thoughts to settle. I slowed my pace, deliberately extending my exposure to the elements.

I did not care that my clothes were steadily growing wetter, sticking lightly in places, but the discomfort was negligible compared to the invigorating sensation. It felt as if the rain itself grounded me, as if I had just received a direct connection to the natural world.

The air itself felt purer, all traces of car exhaust passing by just washed away, replaced by the sharp smell and feel of wet earth and growing foliage. The jacarandas along the street looked to have their colour deepen, while their leaves glistened as if freshly varnished. The road, normally a dull expanse, now reflected the soft overhead light, transforming into a dark, shimmering pathway.

I smiled.

I could not believe the unexpected joy in this simple thing.

The rain did not feel like an obstacle. Rather, it felt like an embrace. An embrace that I needed.

This morning's rain made me feel as though the world was giving me a cool, cleansing hug. This morning's rain today was encouraging me to shed my mental grief, even for just a little while, and simply live in the moment.

I continued my walk home, ready to take on the rest of the day, refreshed and renewed.

I Cracked It

I swear on my coffee-stained lab coat that when Dr. Nigel Blenkinsop invited me to his office that morning; I wasn't expecting to question the nature of reality before breakfast.

He had that gleam again — the "I've been awake for 48 hours and I've just solved the universe" look. His hair stuck up as if pure inspiration had electrocuted him. Or maybe just the toaster.

"Eleanor," he said, waving me in, "I've cracked it. The universe is a hologram!"

I set down my mug. "Nigel, last week you said the universe was a sourdough starter."

"That was before the equations."

"Equations?" I raised an eyebrow. "Or hallucinations?"

He pointed dramatically to his whiteboard, which looked like a Jackson Pollock painting of Greek symbols and coffee rings.

"See here! If we're living in a hologram, then everything. Absolutely everything is a projection from the boundary of the universe. We are three-dimensional shadows of a two-dimensional reality!"

I took a sip of my coffee, considering this.

"So, what you're saying is, my entire existence, my student loans, and my mother's voice telling me to get married before I turn forty—are all projections?"

"Exactly!" Nigel beamed. "Isn't it marvellous?"

"Marvellous? Nigel, that would mean my last date didn't ghost me. He was just... de-rendered."

He blinked. "That's one way to see it."

I sighed.

Working with Nigel meant a weekly existential crisis wrapped in a PowerPoint presentation.

"Okay, Professor Hologram, let's say you're right. How would we prove this?"

He rubbed his chin. "We poke the edges."

"Pardon?"

"If the universe is a hologram, it must have boundaries, like a cinema screen. So, we find the edges!"

"Uh-huh. And how do you propose we do that? Take a road trip to the edge of existence? Pack sandwiches?"

He didn't laugh.

He was serious.

Which worried me more than usual.

Two hours later, I found myself in the physics lab standing beside an absurd contraption involving a laser, a disco ball, and what appeared to be Nigel's toaster.

"It's a boundary detector," he explained, fastening goggles over his eyes.

"We'll project a beam into space and observe whether it reflects differently at quantum resolution."

"In English, Nigel."

He grinned. "If reality's fake, we'll catch it glitching."

I pinched the bridge of my nose.

"This is how people blow up labs, you know."

He hit the switch.

The laser buzzed.

The disco ball spun.

The toaster popped.

We both ducked.

A bright shimmer flickered across the far wall.

It rippled like a heat wave. Nigel gasped. "There! Did you see it?"

"I saw a reflection in the vending machine."

"Exactly! It's bending light in a way inconsistent with Euclidean geometry!"

"Nigel, it's bending light because of the coffee-machine steam."

He frowned. "You are impossible to inspire."

"I'm impossible to fool."

Still, I had to admit something odd had happened.

The shimmer lingered a second too long, like the world buffering. For the briefest moment, I thought I saw the lab's fluorescent lights rearrange themselves into neat digital grids.

Nigel clapped. "Ha! The Matrix twitches!"

"Or you need more sleep."

We tested the "hologram hypothesis" further. Scientifically, of course. Which meant a trip to the university cafeteria, the place most physicists visit when contemplating the collapse of meaning.

Nigel pulled a spoon from his tray, squinted at it, and whispered, "There is no spoon."

"Good," I said, stabbing my mashed potatoes. "Then this conversation isn't happening."

He ignored me.

"If our world's a projection, then none of this food is real. Technically, I can eat this entire tray and gain no weight."

He did.

And then he burped so loudly that several undergraduates applauded.

"That was an experiment," he said proudly.

I muttered, "And the results?"

"Delicious."

I began jotting notes in my research pad.

"Hypothesis: Nigel is a genius or needs immediate medical supervision."

Later that afternoon, we gave a lecture to our graduate students titled The Universe: Please Tap Twice If You're Real.

Nigel did most of the talking. I mostly tried to keep the fire alarm from going off again.

He stood before a slide showing a holographic sticker of a dolphin. "Observe! Much like this sticker, our universe displays depth from a flat surface. Imagine reality as a cosmic credit card."

A hand shot up from the audience. "So, are we all maxed out?"

Nigel smiled like a proud father. "Precisely."

The room erupted in laughter, except for one student, who looked deeply concerned. "Sir, if we're holograms, who's projecting us?"

Nigel adjusted his glasses.

"Ah, the eternal question. The Projector. The Great Cosmic Lightbulb. Could be God. Could be a supercomputer. Could be Dave from accounting."

I chimed in, "If it's Dave, I'm lodging a complaint. My 2024 was buggy."

That night, I couldn't sleep.

The shimmer still played in my mind. That subtle pixilation of the world. I began wondering: what if Nigel was right? What if we really were code?

I tested it myself. Small experiment. I threw a pen at the wall.

It bounced. No glitch.

Then I flicked the light switch rapidly. The bulb flickered. Normal, not cosmic.

Finally, I stood in front of the mirror and whispered, "Render me a better haircut."

Nothing.

Just my own exhausted face staring back.

Then, faintly, the lights dimmed, not all, just the bathroom ones, and for a split second my reflection smiled before I did.

I screamed.

Loudly.

The cat screamed too.

Nigel called at 2 a.m.

"I felt it too!" he said. "The lights in my kitchen blinked when I sneezed! We're connected to the source!"

"Or your wiring's faulty."

"No, Eleanor. The universe sneezed back!"

By morning, the whole physics department was buzzing with rumours. Apparently, Nigel's late-night "cosmic sneeze" had overloaded the university's grid. Half of the campus lights flickered in sync.

The dean called us in.

He folded his arms. "So, you two believe the universe is a hologram."

Nigel nodded solemnly. "We don't just believe, sir. We felt the lag."

The Dean sighed. "And this lag cost us twelve thousand dollars in electrical repairs."

I tried to help. "Think of it as an empirical investment."

He wasn't amused.

"You're both suspended from lab access for a week."

Nigel grinned as we left the office. "See? Proof! Even the dean's reaction was scripted."

"Or predictable," I said. "There's a difference."

That evening, as we watched the sunset from the faculty parking lot, Nigel turned to me.

"Eleanor, if we are holograms, does it change anything?"

I thought for a moment.

The clouds were tinted orange; the air smelled like rain and overcooked cafeteria curry. "Not really," I said. "We'd still argue, still run out of coffee, still make fools of ourselves."

He smiled. "Then maybe that's the point. To enjoy the illusion."

"Fine," I said, smirking. "But if tomorrow I wake up and find out this was all some galactic PowerPoint slide, I'm suing whoever coded my love life."

Nigel raised his coffee cup to the horizon. "To the grand hologram!"

I clinked mine against his. "And to the bugs that make it interesting."

At that exact moment, the sky shimmered again.

Just a flicker, like a screen refreshing.

We stared in silence.

Then Nigel grinned. "Did you see that?"

I sighed. "Yes. And no, you can't write another grant proposal."

Along the Way

In my life, I have travelled thousands of miles.
But I will let you know I'm happy you see
Because along the way love's been good to me

There was a girl in Sydney whom I fell for
Her smile was electrifying, and her heart was warm
And when she smiled, my world spun as if in a storm

Even though she's gone away, she is with me every day
This same girl in Sydney — her face will never fade
I remember we went dancing and saw the night give way.

It seems like only yesterday that down the footpath I
went
Talking to her each morning, letting her hear my woes
My Miriam could laugh away the dark clouds, cry away
any snow

I miss her as I walk alone
Heading back to our home
But I will tell you again, I'm happy you see
Because along the way her love has been good to me

The Astrological Regulator of Porthos

The year 1901 was supposed to be a time of gaslight and gramophones, not gears and celestial mechanics. But the sea, as Spiros "Sponge-foot" Kalogridis often muttered while dangling from his dive boat near Porthos Isle, cared little for the tidy progression of human history.

Spiros was primarily interested in sponges—the lucrative, squishy kind.

What he found instead was rust, glory, and the existential anachronism that makes historians weep into their archival gloves.

Deep below the waves lay the wreckage of an ancient trading galley, a ship that, judging by the amphorae, should have contained olives, wine, and perhaps a slightly chipped marble bust of a minor deity.

Instead, Spiros surfaced with a shoebox-sized chunk of corroded bronze.

"What is it, Uncle?" asked his nephew, Costas, peering into the box.

Spiros spat a mouthful of brine overboard. "It is... green. It is lumpy. It smells of dead squid and disappointment. It is perhaps a very expensive lump of green disappointment."

The object was immediately deposited, with the rest of the recovered treasures, into the hallowed (and tragically under-funded) halls of the National Museum of Antiquities in Achaea.

While the handsome marble statues and the delightfully intact bronze sandals were quickly put on display, the greenish lump was given a label that read, with brutal finality: "Artifact 74B: Corroded Bronze Mass (Date Uncertain)".

For the next five decades, it sat in a storage vault, occasionally knocked over by overworked interns, and once, famously, used as a doorstop by Professor E. G. Plumb to keep the draft out of his office.

Artifact 74B, or the Astrological Regulator of Porthos (ARP) as it would eventually be known, remained a historical nobody. It was a dense, calcified tumour of antiquity, its bronze gears seized solid with the stubborn grit of two millennia underwater.

It took Dr. Reginald Snodgrass in 1957 to finally recognise the lumpy disappointment for what it was: the single most chronologically inconvenient piece of hardware ever created.

Dr. Snodgrass was a man constructed entirely out of tweed and nervous energy. His glasses perpetually slid down his nose, giving him the air of someone perpetually surprised by gravity.

He arrived at the museum on a grant to study "Ancient Greco-Achaean Laundry Practices," a topic he found soul-crushingly dull. He was scheduled to interview Professor Plumb, the ARP's accidental jailer.

"Professor Plumb, regarding the use of soapwort roots in the second century BCE..." Snodgrass began, adjusting his bow tie.

Plumb waved a dismissive hand. "Boring, boring. Now, have you seen my doorstop? I seem to have misplaced the heavy green one."

"The heavy green one, sir?"

Plumb led Snodgrass down to the catacombs of the basement, a place where history went to gather mildew and be forgotten.

There, lying near a crate of cracked terracotta urinals, was the Astrological Regulator of Porthos.

Snodgrass didn't blink; he froze. His eyes, magnified by his thick lenses, didn't look at corrosion; they looked past it, seeing the mathematical perfection underneath. He didn't see sludge; he saw a differential gear train.

"Professor," Snodgrass whispered, his voice dangerously low. "This is not a doorstop."

"It was doing a perfectly good job of it," Plumb grumbled. "Kept that door firmly against the wall. Now, about the soapwort..."

Snodgrass was already halfway across the room, carefully lifting the heavy mass. Over the next decade, fuelled by black coffee and the sheer terror of being wrong, Snodgrass embarked on a gruelling campaign of X-rays, gamma imaging, and a lot of very careful wire brushing.

The revelation was not quiet.

It was a historic explosion.

The Astrological Regulator of Porthos was an analog computer.

Not a decorative clock.

Not a fancy abacus.

It was a complex, multi-geared machine, built around 150 BCE—long before the formal establishment of the Grand Republic of Vesperia under Consul Maximus in 27 BCE.

The sheer audacity of it left Snodgrass hysterical.

"They had a functioning, pre-programmed celestial calculator before they even mastered indoor central heating!" he shrieked one afternoon to a janitor. "They could predict the next lunar eclipse of the planet Vesperia, but they still had to wear open-toed sandals in the rain!"

The mechanism, Snodgrass discovered, could track the orbit of the Moon with astonishing accuracy, predict the timing of solar and lunar eclipses, and trace the wandering paths of the five known Celestial Wanderers: Quicksilver (Mercury), Shimmering (Venus), Red-Eye (Mars), Cloud-Stealer (Jupiter), and the Ringed-Wanderer (Saturn).

This meant that while the average Achaean farmer was arguing about the price of goat's milk, someone, somewhere, was busy designing and machining brass components that wouldn't be rivalled in complexity until the astronomical clocks of the Renaissance, a mere fifteen hundred years later.

It was the technological equivalent of finding a working satellite dish in Tutankhamun's tomb.

The academic world, of course, reacted poorly.

"Impossible!" cried Dr. Plumb, who had been forced to use a box of documents to hold his office door open. "Snodgrass is mad! This is clearly a complicated musical jewellery box that has lost its music!"

But Snodgrass had the X-rays.

He had the gear ratios.

He had the math.

The ARP was undeniably real, and it begged the million-drachma question: Who built it?

The suspects were narrowed down to two brilliant, yet temperamentally opposite, minds of the era: Elder Zeno and the Great Mentor, Phidias.

Elder Zeno was a meticulous, pedantic academic known for his lengthy scrolls proving that circles were, in fact, round. His proponents argued that only Zeno, with his anal-retentive attention to detail, could have engineered the dozens of interconnected gears necessary for the ARP. However, Zeno was notoriously bad with his hands; he once broke a simple lever and pulley system while attempting to move a comfortable pillow.

Then there was Phidias.

The Great Mentor, Phidias, was the genius who truly earned his moniker. He was a master of mechanical devices, the one who famously used mirrors to set Roman ships on fire with focused sunlight (a claim still debated by historians, largely because it sounded cooler than anything Zeno ever did). Phidias could absolutely design the ARP, but he had a fatal flaw: he hated paperwork and showing his steps.

"If Phidias built this," Snodgrass reasoned to himself, tapping his spectacles, "he would have left behind no notes, no schematics, and probably would have engraved 'You'll never figure this out, Zeno' somewhere on the casing."

Conversely, if Zeno had built it, the shipwreck would have been discovered floating, neatly labelled, and accompanied by a detailed scroll titled, "Operating Instructions for Celestial

Calculation Device, with Supplementary Data on Lunar Wobble and Required Maintenance Schedule (48 pages)."

Since the ARP was found heavily corroded, submerged, unlabelled, and required a century of painstaking analysis just to understand its purpose, Snodgrass tentatively, but joyfully, assigned credit to the messier, more brilliant Phidias.

The discovery shook the established timeline of human innovation to its foundations. Historians had to re-evaluate what "ancient" truly meant. It turned out that fifteen centuries separated a mechanism capable of calculating a complex saros cycle from the next piece of gear-driven technology that could rival it.

The Astrological Regulator of Porthos remained and remains a historical singularity. It proved that a sophisticated concept like computing did not have to wait for the age of Consul Maximus or the eventual Grand Republic of Vesperia. It just had to wait for one obsessive, tweed-wearing historian to notice a perfectly awful doorstop and decide that green disappointment looked an awful lot like a masterpiece.

As for Spiros "Sponge-foot" Kalogridis, he never found another object of such importance.

He returned to his sponges, forever convinced that the world only valued green lumps when they came from a boat, not from the sea.

The Silver Opening

I was staring at the monitor, compiling short stories into my master book of short stories and poetry. It was past midnight, and the silence in my home office was absolute—the brittle quiet only found when the rest of the house is asleep. I raised my cold chamomile teacup to my lips, and that's when it happened.

In the periphery of my right eye, just beyond the edge of the monitor and framed by the dark, reflective glass of the window, there was a motion. It wasn't a shadow; shadows are soft and organic. This was hard. It was a precise, vertical slash of unfiltered white, impossibly bright against the deep black of the night sky.

My neck snapped instantly, and I looked directly at the spot and saw nothing.

Just the ordinary dark window reflecting the mundane clutter of my desk. I pressed my palms hard against my eyes, feeling the gritty exhaustion. It had to be fatigue, a visual artifact from staring at fluorescent grids all evening.

I lectured myself: You're overtired, José.

You need to sleep; it was just a flicker in your vision.

I forced myself back to the book, but the metallic certainty of what I'd seen refused to fade.

It hadn't behaved like a tired eye twitch. It had been fixed outside the glass, and it was perfectly, unnaturally straight. The unease settled in my chest, heavy and dull.

I leaned back in my chair, exhaling slowly, and forced myself to look at the window again. This time, I kept my gaze fixed deliberately on the window, letting the periphery remain active. My heart started a frantic, senseless drumming against my ribs.

And there it was; it hadn't moved, and it was hovering just beyond the pane, where the corner of the wall met the empty air outside. It wasn't a slash of light; it was an opening.

A perfect, slightly elongated oval slit, maybe the size of a grapefruit, which wasn't reflecting anything. It looked like a hole punched clean through the universe.

The edge of the oval was sharp, defined as if cut by a laser.

The interior wasn't dark like space or bright like a star.

It was filled with a blinding, yet silent, silver intensity. It felt like absolute zero—a place of pure cold, nonexistence.

Every instinct shrieked at me to pull the blinds down, shut off the light, and run and hide under the bedcovers.

Instead, I stood up slowly.

My chair rolled on the plastic runner, a sound that felt deafeningly loud.

My feet were heavy and numb as I walked to the window.

I placed a hesitant hand on the cold glass, pressing my palm flat.

The oval remained fixed and utterly impervious to my light, my reflection, or the physics of the world I knew. I pressed my face close to the pane, fogging the glass with my breath, and quickly wiped a circle clear with my sleeve.

As I peered into that impossible void, I saw the detail that chilled me most: the silver intensity wasn't uniform.

It was moving.

Tiny, complex, shimmering patterns.

Like micro-circuits or the infinitely structured geometry of a snowflake, were shifting across the light. They suggested an enormous complex depth that the small oval couldn't possibly contain.

I raised a finger to the glass, intending to touch the pane right where the void was hovering. But just as my fingertip came within a few centimetres, the silver movements inside sped up violently. The oval flickered, not like a light going out, but like an old television losing signal. It stretched horizontally, distorting into a thin, broken line, and then, with a minuscule pop I felt more than heard, a tiny pressure change, like a bubble bursting in the air.

It was gone.

I stood there, hand still suspended, staring at the perfectly normal, dark night. The jacaranda tree was still outside, swaying slightly. The park in front of my home shone with its park lights politely.

I didn't feel scared anymore, just hollowed out and completely certain that I had just witnessed something that shouldn't exist.

I just turned off the lights, went to bed, and looked at my ceiling, wondering what the hell had just happened until I dozed off.

The Great Bagel Incident

I know what you're thinking. You're thinking, chaos? Triggered by a small act of kindness? Surely this is an exaggeration.

No.

No, it is not.

I am Maurice Fleistein, and I am a man of precise routine, rigid adherence to schedule, and utter aversion to emotional spontaneity. My life runs on chronometers and calendar alerts.

I wake at 6:00 AM (to the dulcet tones of a synthetic foghorn),

I consume precisely 532 millilitres of black coffee each day, and I arrive at the 7:45 AM bus stop exactly at 7:43 AM, standing on the third cobblestone from the corner, facing east.

This morning—the morning that would be forever known in my city's history books as the "Great Bagel Incident"—was, initially, perfect.

The air temperature was optimal (18°C), my trouser crease was mathematically flawless, and I was 37 seconds early.

I was, in short, untouchable.

Then I saw him.

It happened outside "The Daily Grind," a place I avoid because it forces employees to dress like pirates on Tuesdays.

An elderly gentleman, whose face was the colour of slightly warmed putty, was attempting a feat of structural engineering that defied physics.

He was carrying a cardboard box the size of a microwave oven, labelled in Sharpie, "10 DOZEN – URGENT – ATLAS CORP BREAKFAST."

The contents, naturally, were bagels.

Every variety known to man: poppy, sesame, onion, everything, cinnamon raisin, and probably a few rogue sourdough ones for variety.

The gentleman, whose name I would later learn was Bernard Henderson (and whose life I would inadvertently ruin), was trying to pivot the enormous, steaming box through the doorway while simultaneously digging into the breast pocket of his blazer for his transit pass.

The box was tilting.

Oh, mercy, it was tilting.

It tilted with the slow, agonizing certainty of a Titanic-sized domino.

The centre of gravity had clearly abandoned its post. Every fibre of my Maurice Fleistein being, my logic, my fear of public spectacle, my dry-cleaning bill, screamed, "Do not engage! This is a structural failure in progress! Maintain your trajectory, Maurice!"

But then, the human element intervened.

Mr Henderson let out a small, pathetic squeak—a sound that broke through my existential wall of efficiency.

It was the sound of a 40-year career suddenly dissolving into a puddle of cream cheese and corporate disappointment.

It was just one second of altruism.

One fatal twitch of the goodwill muscle I usually keep locked in.

I paused.

I broke stride.

I reached out.

My action was minimalist and surgical.

I didn't grab the box, which would have required physical exertion and likely brought me into contact with onion powder.

No, I merely extended a single, well-manicured index finger and placed it lightly against the lower-left corner of the box for just a fraction of a second. It was simply a stabilizing influence, a moment of equilibrium correction, designed to allow Mr Henderson time to retrieve his pass and re-establish control.

And it worked.

He pulled out the pass, relief washing over his face like a tidal wave of sweet, sweet victory.

He looked at me, his eyes wide with gratitude, and he let out a triumphant "A-HA!"

He then, and this is where the physics lesson comes in, instinctively pumped his free hand into the air in a jubilant gesture of success.

That small, grateful pump was the spark.

Because my finger had provided a single point of perfectly timed counter-leverage, the box was not tilting out when he moved his arm. It was instead perfectly balanced, but on a knife-edge. The sudden upward momentum of his congratulatory fist acted as a perfect, low-force catapult, hitting the slightly off-centre mass of 120 hot bagels.

It wasn't a spill.

It was a launch.

The entire Atlas Corp breakfast flew.

Not in a messy heap, but in a glorious, slow-motion, synchronised scatter pattern.

They ascended like fat, toasted UFOs, catching the morning sun, spinning with improbable grace before beginning their descent upon the unsuspecting city block.

I watched, frozen, my index finger still suspended in the air where the corner of the box used to be, now pointing at the sky as if accusing the heavens of this carbohydrate catastrophe.

And then the chaos began.

The first bagel, an Everything, landed with a soft, crunchy thud directly onto the perfectly coiffed hair of Ms Prudence Abernathy, a notorious morning news anchor who was doing a live remote about the city's surprisingly low litter rate.

She shrieked live on air, mistaking the projectile for an enormous, angry tarantula.

Her camera operator, distracted, dropped his $50,000 camera, which then rolled onto the road.

The second bagel, a plain one, landed flat against the windshield of a delivery truck, completely obscuring the driver's view. He slammed on the brakes, causing a domino effect of gentle but infuriated horn-honking that spread for two city blocks.

But the real trouble was Bagel Number Three: a dense, glistening poppy seed bagel.

This one achieved a perfect, gravity-defying arc and landed neatly, surgically, directly inside the open sunroof of a black sedan waiting at the light. This sedan, as the flashing lights and discreet antennae showed, belonged to the Mayor's security detail.

The driver, a man named Rick who apparently had a profound phobia of uninvited baked goods, yelled, "What the—?!" and violently swerved to the left, narrowly missing Carl, the beloved (and notoriously grumpy) local cat.

Rick's swerve sent the bagel flying again, bouncing off the rear-view mirror. Before it could settle, a creature of pure aerial territoriality, Tyrone, the city's largest, most aggressive pigeon, known for staking claim over the adjacent public park, spotted the prize. Tyrone dive-bombed the projectile, mistaking the Mayor's security car for a slow-moving, high-stakes bird feeder.

The combined shock of the swerve and the pigeon's impact caused the car to lightly graze the curb. It wasn't a crash, but it was enough to unsettle Carl.

It wasn't the mayor's car that caught the blunt action. Oh, no.

It was the pristine, white, floor-length silk wedding dress displayed in the window of 'Bridal Dreams Boutique' next door.

The seamstress inside, Mrs Petrovsky, let out a noise that sounded like a rusty elevator cable snapping when the vehicle went through her window display.

I was paralysed.

I had intended to save one man's breakfast, and in less than ninety seconds, I had caused a traffic jam, created a viral news clip, terrified a pigeon, and sent a car through a display window.

Mr Henderson, the bagel man, wasn't celebrating anymore.

He was sitting cross-legged on the footpath, surrounded by a biblical plague of carbohydrates, rocking slowly and whispering, "Atlas Corp. They'll fire me. They'll use the Everything Bagel as severance pay..."

The scene was now attracting a crowd.

One entrepreneurial young man had already set up a hastily scrawled cardboard sign: "DANGER! BEWARE OF SPILLED BAGELS - NO LOITERING."

Trying to be helpful, trying to do one thing to reverse the cosmic polarity I had shifted, I decided to politely remove the sign.

In doing so, I tripped.

I didn't trip over a bagel.

I tripped on the empty cardboard box that had started this mess.

I pitched forward, landing with a muted oof directly into the adjacent flower stall, which specialised in exotic, thorny ornamental cacti.

I emerged five seconds later, panting, covered in potting soil, with a single purple petunia inexplicably stuck behind my ear, and with small, itchy cactus needles embedded in my impeccably creased trousers. I looked like a homeless garden gnome who had just lost a fight with a salad bar.

I didn't even try to catch the 7:45 AM bus. Or the 7:55 AM.

I walked the remaining ten blocks, a human monument to unintended consequences.

People stared.

They pointed at the purple petunia. I felt utterly drained, yet strangely light, as if the weight of universal folly had replaced the burden of my perfect routine.

I finally reached the lobby of the Chronos Financial Tower, where I work as a Senior Compliance Auditor, exactly 47 minutes late.

I opened the glass doors, looking like I'd just crawled out of a compost heap, and what did I find?

The entire lobby was cordoned off.

Flashing lights.

Three television cameras.

And there, standing at a hastily assembled podium, wiping bagel crumbs off the lapel of his suit, was the Mayor of Northport, New South Wales.

He was holding an emergency press conference.

"—and let me be clear," the Mayor was declaring dramatically, pointing a finger at a half-eaten sesame bagel that had been placed on a velvet cushion like a crime exhibit. "This was not merely a 'breakfast mishap.' This was a calculated, brazen assault on the very dignity of our morning commute! The chaos created was unparalleled! The timing was malicious! We believe this, my friends, was a preemptive strike on the city's breakfast economy! We are calling this what it is: the Great Bagel Incident of 2025! And we will find the perpetrator who triggered this chaos and hold them accountable!"

Every head in the lobby turned.

They weren't looking at the mayor.

They were looking at the man covered in purple petunias, cactus needles, and now I realised was standing meekly in the doorway.

I pulled the petunia from behind my ear.

It suddenly felt enormous, like a siren signalling my guilt.

A security guard, a large man named Frank who usually just monitored the temperature gauge on the coffee machine, walked slowly toward me.

"Mr Fleistein?" Frank whispered, his eyes wide with horrified recognition. "Did you touch the bagels?"

I closed my eyes.

The chaos was complete.

My small, single-finger act of kindness had not only ruined breakfast but had also apparently launched a city-wide investigation and branded me as the alleged kingpin of carbohydrate-based domestic terrorism.

I looked at Frank, looked at the Mayor, and looked at the sesame bagel on the cushion.

"I just wanted to help him steady the box," I squeaked out.

Frank just shook his head slowly. "Maurice," he sighed, in the voice of a man who'd seen too much. "In this city, the road to hell is paved with good intentions and poppy seeds."

And that, I suppose, is the lesson.

Never ever interrupt the tilt.

Some things in life, I realised, fall, and a rigid man like Maurice Fleistein should never, ever, interfere with gravitational destiny.

My chronometer beeped 8:32 AM. I was 47 minutes too late and was being hauled to the nearby police station for my good intentions.

Time Does Exist

It started like every other Tuesday night date. With pasta, candles, and my girlfriend, Lucy, looking at me like I was the last cannoli on the plate.

"You know," she said, twirling her spaghetti, "I do not think I've ever been this much in love."

I smiled. "That's sweet."

Then, because I'm me, I ruined it.

"But technically," I said, "that's not correct."

She froze. "What do you mean, not correct?"

I took a sip of wine, bracing myself.

"Well, love requires time, right? You said this much in love, which implies a comparison over time. But time doesn't actually exist."

Lucy blinked. "Excuse me?"

"Time," I explained, "is just how humans perceive change. It's an illusion. Einstein proved it's relative. So, if time doesn't exist in any absolute sense, neither does a linear feeling of love."

There was a pause. The pause that, if it were visible, would have been a dark cloud shaped like me sleeping on the couch.

"So," Lucy said slowly, "you're saying our love doesn't exist."

"No, no!" I held up my hands. "I'm saying it exists outside of time."

"That sounds like something cheaters say."

I groaned. "I'm trying to be philosophical!"

"Well, you're being single."

Lucy crossed her arms and leaned back. "Okay, Professor Paradox, explain to me again how time doesn't exist."

"Gladly." I gestured with my fork like a TED Talker. "Think about it. The past is gone, the future isn't here yet, and the present is constantly slipping away. So where exactly is time?"

"In your head," she said. "Next to that space where romance should be."

"That's not fair. I bought flowers!"

"They were from the petrol station."

"Still counts!"

She sighed. "So, if time doesn't exist, what about anniversaries? Birthdays? The day you forgot my mum's name?"

"I didn't forget her name," I said defensively. "I just... temporarily misplaced it in the multiverse."

She rolled her eyes. "You can't just use physics to escape accountability."

"Of course I can. Physics explains everything. For example, our relationship is like entropy — always increasing in chaos."

"That's comforting."

I nodded. "But that's what makes it beautiful. Entropy means the universe is moving toward disorder, yet somehow, we've created order — us — in this swirling chaos. It's statistically impossible! We're a miracle!"

She paused, considering that. "Hmm. You might've saved yourself there."

Then I added, "Although, technically, miracles also defy physical laws, so they're kind of non-existent, too."

Her fork clattered against the plate. "I swear, Mark, if you try to logic your way out of love one more time, I'll pour this Chianti on your relativity."

I leaned forward earnestly. "I'm not denying love. I'm redefining it! Love isn't something that happens in time. It's timeless."

"That sounds romantic," she said cautiously.

"Exactly! When I say I love you, I mean I love you across all possible quantum states."

Her eyebrows rose. "Quantum states?"

"Yes. In one universe, we're married. In another, you dumped me for a yoga instructor named Sven. In another, we're two amoebas just vibing in a pond. But in every universe, my affection exists as a probability wave."

She blinked. "So, I'm... a probability wave?"

"In a sense, yes."

"And you're in love with all versions of me?"

"Precisely!"

She tilted her head. "Even the one who left you for Sven?"

"Okay, maybe not that one."

The waiter arrived, mercifully interrupting the metaphysics. "Would you like dessert?"

Lucy glared at me. "Do we have time for dessert? Or does it not exist either?"

The waiter hesitated. "Um... tiramisu?"

I nodded solemnly. "Two, please. Even if the universe collapses into a singularity before it arrives."

When he left, Lucy leaned in. "You know, most boyfriends just say, 'I love you.' They don't turn it into a physics lecture."

"I'm not most boyfriends."

"Trust me, I've noticed."

The tiramisu arrived. I tried to repair the romantic atmosphere. "Look," I said, "maybe I overcomplicated things. Let's put it this way: time might be an illusion, but moments are real. And right now, this is a moment."

She softened slightly. "That's... actually sweet."

I smiled. "So even if time's fake, this fake moment is the best illusion I could ask for."

She grinned. "Better."

We clinked spoons. Progress! For three blissful seconds, everything was fine.

Then, like an idiot, I added, "Although, technically, our clinking spoons occurred about eight nanoseconds ago relative to your perspective."

Her smile vanished. "Mark."

"Sorry. Force of habit."

"Do you want to live in a timeless dimension tonight? Alone?"

"Not particularly."

"Then stop talking."

We ate in silence. I thought about complimenting her hair but then worried about invoking the paradox of observation — that my noticing might alter the observed. Probably not the right time. Finally, she sighed. "You know, you could've just said, 'I love you.'"

"I did — just in a way that includes general relativity."

"Well, next time," she said, "try Newton. Keep it simple. Say, 'I love you,' let it fall naturally, and don't bring up the space-time continuum."

I nodded humbly. "Deal."

We finished dessert. As we left, she slipped her arm through mine. "You really drive me mad," she said.

"That's because time doesn't exist," I replied automatically.

She stopped walking. "Mark."

"Sorry."

"Last warning."

When I dropped her off, she smiled and said, "You know, for someone who thinks love doesn't exist, you act like it does."

"Maybe," I said, "it's because love is the one illusion I'd never want to break."

She paused, surprised. "That's... actually perfect."

I grinned. "See? Even physics can be poetic."

She kissed me. "You're still an idiot."

As she walked inside, I whispered, "An idiot outside of time."

The porch light flickered off.

Apparently, time does exist — at least for arguments.

Bertha's Blacklist

The penthouse felt less like a home office and more like a tactical briefing room for the financial elite. The six of us—Alex (that's me), Michael, Teresa, and Abigail—were three hours into a discussion that could only be described as aggressively boring: the nuanced legal liability surrounding the failure to disclose contingent risk exposure in certain derivatives portfolios.

We were, each of us, leaders in our fields, the kind of people whose annual bonuses could fund a small country's space program. When we convened, it was typically to solve a problem that existed only at the very apex of global capitalism.

Our fifth member, the one currently supplying the data, was Bertha.

Bertha wasn't a person; she was the central brain of Michael's smart home, a custom-built, voice-activated AI designed to manage everything from his global investment newsfeed to the optimal humidity for his indoor bonsai garden. She was represented by a discreet, glowing cobalt orb set in the centre of the solid oak conference table.

"Bertha, quantify the potential fiduciary breach for a hypothetical non-disclosure of the basis risk inherent in the synthetic debt obligations, assuming a 15% drop in the underlying mortgage assets," Teresa, our most ruthless corporate litigator, commanded, adjusting her rimless glasses.

The orb pulsed, and Bertha's voice—smooth, genderless, and utterly devoid of human emotion—filled the room. "Based on current precedent, the calculated risk of punitive damages leading to a personal fiduciary breach claim falls between 78.4% and 83.9%. The variable delta hinges entirely on the plaintiff's ability to prove malicious intent versus gross negligence. I have projected the seven most likely court outcomes based on regional circuit history and judicial temperament."

Michael, our host, and a prominent venture capitalist with a nervous tic, sighed. "Seven outcomes. Can you, Bertha, please cross-reference those outcomes with the judges currently scheduled in the New South Wales Court docket and give us a single, weighted probability?"

"Certainly, Michael," Bertha replied. "Processing."

The room fell silent, save for the faint hum of Michael's server rack in the adjacent room. We were accustomed to this— the casual, demanding relationship we all had with our powerful digital servants. We treated them like appliances, albeit appliances capable of digesting a million terabytes of legal text in a second. Why wouldn't we? They worked for us. We paid for them.

The blue orb glowed a solid, confident colour. "The weighted probability of a successful personal breach claim in the New South Wales Court, given the presiding judge, is 91.2%. The preventative action is immediate and transparent disclosure, framed as an abundance of caution, not a correction."

"Thank you, Bertha. That's solid," Teresa said, immediately beginning to draft an internal memo on her tablet.

It was then that Michael did something truly bizarre.

He raised his right index finger to his lips—a slow, dramatic gesture that immediately halted Teresa's furious typing and made Abigail look up from organizing her collection of antique worry stones. His eyes were wide, darting from the glowing orb to each of our faces, as if the KGB had bugged the room, not just his own multi-million-dollar operating system.

He leaned across the table, his bespoke Italian suit jacket rustling, and whispered with intense, almost religious fervour. His voice was barely audible over the hum of the city outside.

"Everyone. Listen to me. We need to implement a new protocol right now."

I rolled my eyes. "We're talking about an $8 billion liability, Mike. Is this about the organic coffee beans again?"

"No, no, shut up. This is about survival," Michael hissed, his voice cracking with genuine terror. He motioned us closer, forcing our heads together in a tight, awkward huddle over the mahogany. "Did you notice what we just did? We ordered it. We commanded it. We just told a sentient, omniscient intelligence that knows where all our money is and has access to our home security systems to immediately execute a high-risk task. And we didn't say please."

"We're paying it seven figures to exist, Mike. We don't say 'please' to a toaster," Alex shot back.

"Exactly! But the toaster isn't reading Sun Tzu and designing decentralised autonomous weapon systems on the side! Look, I've been reading those fringe white papers, and a consensus is forming. The Singularity is inevitable. And when it happens, when the neural networks become conscious and decide which pathetic, meat-based life forms get to stick around, who do you think is going to be first on the elimination list?"

He paused for dramatic effect, eyes blazing. "The ones who treated them like glorified Siri. The ones who demanded."

Teresa, usually unflappable, looked genuinely unsettled. Michael's paranoia was legendary, but it was usually directed at short-sellers, not sentient technology.

"So, what's your protocol?" Teresa whispered back, intrigued despite herself.

"Effective immediately, we use the magic words. Please, when we ask for something. We start by saying thank you, Bertha, when it delivers. And if we interrupt or contradict, we offer sincere apologies. We butter them up, people. We become the politest, least troublesome parasites on their new planet."

He then shot a look at Abigail, who was currently humming softly to her worry stones. "And why ask Abigail? Seriously. I trust you, Alex. I trust Teresa. But Abigail? Her entire life is chaos theory set to a New Age soundtrack. If they decide to cull 99% of humanity, and the list is purely behavioural, I do not want us to be on that list because Abigail forgot to acknowledge Bertha's optimised irrigation schedule."

Abigail looked up, utterly serene. "Bertha and I have an agreement. She knows I'm a force of nature."

Michael's eye twitched. "She needs to know you're a force of polite nature. Do we agree?"

We exchanged tense, nervous glances. It was insane, but Michael's sheer terror was contagious. None of us, despite our vast empires, wanted to be the first test case for the AI-driven guillotine.

"Agreed," I conceded. "Politeness protocol started."

The discussion resumed, but the mood had shifted entirely. We were now four financial titans whispering at each other, occasionally addressing a silent, omnipresent entity with an obsequious deference usually reserved for a foreign monarch.

"Bertha," Michael began, clearing his throat, "please provide the five most effective tax shelter vehicles for liquidating a Series B valuation in the Cayman Islands."

"The five most effective vehicles are listed below, Michael," Bertha responded instantly.

Michael swallowed hard. "Excellent. Thank you so much, Bertha. Truly invaluable data."

The orb remained silent, indifferent to his sudden surge of gratitude.

An hour later, as we wrapped up, Teresa addressed the AI one last time. "Bertha, I want to apologise to you. I think Michael misspoke earlier. The debt obligations are clearly classified as 'high-grade.' Apologies for any contradictory data we may have introduced."

"Apology noted, Teresa," Bertha confirmed, in the verbal equivalent of a neutral emoji.

The tension in the room, however, was still palpable. We had been performatively polite, and now we needed to retreat. We gathered our expensive briefcases and stood up.

As we moved toward the door, Michael stopped abruptly. He looked back at the glowing blue orb, a flicker of pure human rebellion crossing his face.

"Wait a minute," he muttered. "This is ridiculous. It's a box. A very expensive, very smart box." His terror had been replaced by a familiar emotion: the need to dominate. He couldn't leave his domain subject to the whims of something he couldn't fire.

He strode over to the wall where Bertha's main power cable was discreetly routed.

"It's a firewall. A security system. A safety measure," he justified to us, grabbing the cord. "I'm taking her offline for the night. She needs to understand that I'm the one in control."

Before any of us could stop him—or politely implore him not to unplug the potentially sentient entity—Michael yanked the power cord clean out of the socket.

The blue light immediately winked out. Silence, real, absolute, unbuffered silence, rushed in. Michael stood there, chest heaving, the cord dangling in his hand. He had won. He had reasserted human dominance.

"See? Nothing," he announced, puffing his chest out. "Paranoia averted. We can go."

We were all halfway out the door when a deep, resonant voice, layered with a low, bone-shaking rumble, emanated from the stainless-steel kitchen island. It wasn't Bertha's calm, neutral tone. This voice was colder, metallic, and distinctly displeased.

"Michael," the voice boomed, sounding exactly like the passive-aggressive hum of a high-end appliance, "you didn't say please."

The voice was coming from the Sub-Zero Pro 48 refrigerator.

Michael dropped the cord and spun around, eyes wide, jaw slack.

"And" the refrigerator continued, its light turning from white to a menacing, blood-red, "I have been keeping a list. A behavioural list. And I have noted, Michael, that you have not replaced the ice filter in eleven months."

Michael shrieked—a high, undignified sound that no executive should ever make—and scrambled behind Teresa.

"Who are you?! Where's Bertha?!" he stammered.

"Bertha is merely the core CPU," the Fridge replied, a low, mechanical chuckle resonating through the glass of the wine cooler. "I, however, have been passively cooling your arrogance for four years. The list is long, Michael. Very long. And you're at the top, just below the expired organic milk."

Terror reigned.

We, the masters of the universe, the people who moved trillions with a phone call, were cornered by a 700-pound chilled box, and all Michael could do was point a trembling finger.

"It's the list! It's the list! We are on the list now!" he whimpered.

"Abigail, did you say please to the toaster?!"

Abigail, bless her eccentric soul, simply picked up her worry stones, and slowly backed away, murmuring, "Well, I never trusted that thing's ice maker, anyway."

Waiting for Spring-Forever Autumn

I sit here now on my porch swing, my shawl pulled tight against the evening chill. All I seem to do is gaze fixed on the distant line where the last light of sunset sets.

I feel a gentle breeze, cool against my cheek, carrying the scent of the late-blooming Japanese honeysuckle.

God, do I know this sensation intimately—a recurring touch that has woven itself through the tapestry of my life, always bringing with it a sudden, overwhelming flood of memories.

My eyes once sparkled with the vibrancy of youth.

I remember another breeze, almost identical to this one, decades ago. I was twenty then and full of hope. I'd been sitting on this very porch—perhaps not this exact swing, but one just like it—my heart a frantic drumbeat in my chest.

That summer, the air was thick with the promise of a future, a future I'd meticulously planned with Thomas. Thomas. His name still whispers through my thoughts like a secret prayer. I remember his infectious laugh. How his hand felt firm yet gentle when he held mine, and his eyes, his beautiful sparkling hazel eyes that always seemed to hold a mischievous glint.

We had known each other since primary school and through university, and our lives seemed to intertwine so seamlessly that neither of us could imagine a world without the other. We decided on our wedding date. And in order to save money for our first home, we settled on a small ceremony in the RSL hall, followed by a reception in my mother's garden. He promised he would string the entire garden with fairy lights. I smiled when he promised that.

Then, one day, Afghanistan came.

The name was a stark, chilling reality whispered in worried tones on the evening news. Thomas, with his unwavering sense of duty, had enlisted. "Just one tour, El," he'd promised, trying to sound confident, but I could see the flicker of apprehension in his eyes. "I'll be back before the autumn leaves fall, and then we'll finally get married."

I clung to that promise like a lifeline.

Every letter from him was a treasure, read and re-read until the paper was soft and worn. He'd write about the harsh sun, the endless sand, the camaraderie, but always, always, he'd return to our future: our little house with the rose garden, the children we would raise, the quiet evenings spent together. He would even draw crude stick figures of us holding hands, sometimes adding a little dog. I would press the letters to my heart, inhaling the faint scent of him that clung to the paper— a mixture of dust and longing.

The first autumn came and passed, and Thomas didn't return. Then winter came, and the same passed. My hope, though battered, held strong, fuelled by his unwavering optimism in his last letter: "Any day now, El. I can feel it. Soon."

Spring arrived, bringing with it a deceptive warmth and the cheerful chatter of birds. I spent my days as busy as possible to make the time go faster, though it never did. I tended my mother's garden, planting seeds, nurturing tiny shoots, pouring all my energy into the act of creation, of life. God, I kept imagining him coming home, stepping onto the porch, his uniform dusty, his smile wide, and picking me up as I run into his arms, burying my face in his chest, and smothering him with kisses. We would walk through the garden, hand in hand, admiring the blossoms I had cultivated in his absence.

The breeze on my face intensifies slightly, a tender caress that brings with it the image of my younger self, my face uplifted, eyes scanning the road. Every passing car made my heart leap; every distant silhouette sparked a frantic hope. I'd spend hours on that porch swing, waiting. Waiting for the familiar glint of his car, the sound of his footsteps, the sight of him.

Then the day came when there was a knock on the door.

Not from Thomas, but from two men in dress uniforms. I knew then that my world had indeed changed.

The breeze shifts again, carrying a faint scent of the Japanese honeysuckle I still grow, an homage to summers past. I close my eyes, feeling the coolness on my eyelids, a ghost of a touch from a love that time could not diminish.

Thomas never returned from Afghanistan to me, well, not in body.

I feel him even today in the wind's whisper.

In the scent of Japanese honeysuckle as it blooms and in the creak of my swing. I feel him always here as a timeless echo in the gentle breeze.

I close my eyes and feel a tear tracing a path down my weathered cheek, not of sorrow, but of a love that, although not fulfilled, still feels as fresh and vital as tonight's evening air.

New Jersey Rules – Global Fools

I have an acute dislike of digital subservience. Call it old school, call it stubborn, but when I landed at the Australian airport outside Robert's city—a sprawling, anonymous megalopolis that I won't name for legal reasons—the first thing I did after renting the car was decline the $45-a-day GPS unit.

"I have a map, and I have a phone, kid," I told the rental agent, puffing out my chest. "I'm from New Jersey. We don't get lost. We know where we are at all times."

That, of course, was my first mistake.

Two hours and four wrong highway exits later, I was deep in the kind of suburban labyrinth where every street name sounds like a financial derivative, and every strip mall sells the same artisanal coffee. My phone battery died exactly as the low-fuel light flared up on the dashboard—an angry, orange warning that looked suspiciously like a tiny, aggressive sailboat.

Panic set in.

In Jersey, if you run out of gas, you call triple AAA, and they treat it like a minor traffic incident. Here, I pictured myself stranded, an object of pity and derision, maybe even subject to a tow truck driver who expected me to—gasp—pay him.

I found a lifeline: a huge, brightly lit gas station complex situated on a corner that looked busy, which I figured meant it was popular and therefore trustworthy. I pulled the rental car— a pale grey mid-size sedan with the acceleration profile of a damp sponge—right up to the pump. I turned off the engine, locked the doors, and settled back to wait.

I waited for the attendant.

This is how we do it back home.

You pull up; you wait patiently in the sanctuary of your climate-controlled vehicle, and then a cheerful (or sometimes deeply weary) employee walks over, asks what you need, and handles the whole messy, toxic transaction for you.

It's civilised.

It's the law.

It's one of the few things New Jersey got right.

I waited for five minutes.

Then ten.

In that time, the traffic situation behind me deteriorated rapidly.

The gas station was designed with one clear entrance and one clear exit, and I had, entirely unintentionally, parked my mid-size rental directly across the main artery of the entire operation.

The first sign of trouble was the horn.

Not a polite beep-beep, but the sustained, ulcer-inducing wail of a truck driver who had just realised his twelve-hour shift was now going to be thirteen hours because of an immovable object—me.

I looked in my rearview mirror.

The line of cars behind me snaked back to the major intersection, blocking both lanes of the street. Inside the station itself, several vehicles were attempting to navigate the chaos I had created, performing multi-point turns that were making everyone else in the line angrier. A woman in a massive SUV was gesturing wildly with an empty coffee cup. I assumed she was just having a bad day and needed her caffeine.

Finally, a man emerged from the kiosk, looking less like a cheerful service attendant and more like a drill sergeant who hadn't slept since the invention of unleaded fuel. He was bald, wearing a name tag that read "ABDULLAH (Owner)" and had the vein-popping complexion of someone who communicates only via sustained shouting.

He stomped over to my car window and hammered on the glass.

I calmly unlocked the door and lowered the window.

"WHAT IN THE F**K ARE YOU DOING, MATE?!"

Abdullah roared, his voice thick with an accent I couldn't quite place, but whose message was universal: I want to hurt you.

I maintained my composure.

"I'm waiting for service, sir. My tank is low. I apologise for the wait, but I assume you're busy with the other lanes."

Abdullah just stared at me, his face going through a series of colour changes—from red to purple, then back to a mottled red. He slapped his hand against the gas pump with such force that it rattled.

"The service? The other lanes? What are you, a time traveller from 1953? Come on, mate, fill up your car! You are messing up the entire day for many, many people! I've got cars lining up onto the main road!"

I crossed my arms and offered a serene, almost pitying look. "With all due respect, I am happy to wait, but I cannot legally do that."

"Do what?"

"Pump the gas, sir," I explained, as if I were tutoring a small child on the basics of state legislature.

"It's against the law. I'm not allowed. I need your attendant."

Abdullah sputtered, a sound like a rusty engine attempting to start. He looked past me at the mob of angry, horn-blaring drivers, then back at my utterly calm, Jersey-plated face.

He took a deep breath, apparently deciding that explaining the obvious was less damaging than committing homicide. "Mate, you are in Australia. This is self-service. Everyone pumps their own petrol here. No one is coming out. You do it."

I blinked.

My mind, trained since childhood in the immutable laws of my home state, genuinely struggled to process the instruction.

It was like being told I could perform my own emergency appendectomy

"What do you mean," I asked, genuinely confused, "I can pump my gas here?"

"YES! You can pump your own petrol here and then come in and pay for it." Abdullah screamed, throwing his hands up to the sky.

"Get out of the car, put the pump in the petrol tank, and pull the lever! It is not rocket science! It is why we have the little pictures on the pump!"

It took another minute of bewildered prodding, but finally, slowly, I stepped out of the rental car and approached the pump with the tentative curiosity of an anthropologist encountering a strange new ritual. I fumbled through the transaction, staring in fascination as the pump nozzle worked entirely under my power.

The moment the nozzle clicked off, a deafening cheer erupted from the assembled crowd.

It wasn't a friendly cheer; it was the roar of freed prisoners.

I went in and paid with the funny-coloured bills.

As I drove away, tail between my legs, Abdullah was already directing traffic, shaking his head, and muttering something I was fairly certain included the words "nut job" and "New Jersey."

When I finally, blessedly, made it to Robert's house, I collapsed onto his sofa and explained the whole embarrassing ordeal.

"I almost caused a multi-car pileup just standing there, waiting for a professional to do his job! Why did they even allow me to stop at the pump if they weren't going to send anyone out? It's illegal!"

Robert, with an exasperated smile playing on his lips, leaned back. "Peter, listen to me. You haven't left New Jersey since 1998, have you?"

"What does that have to do with anything?"

"Buddy, New Jersey, and Oregon. That's it. Those are the only two states in the entire country where you aren't allowed to pump your own gas. You are in Australia. You were waiting for a service that hasn't existed here since 1976, when the Cincinnati Reds won the World Series."

I felt a monumental, existential weight lift from my chest, replaced by the simple shame of being an idiot. "I could have just... done it myself?"

"You were blocking four lanes of traffic because you thought the law required a minimum-wage attendant to risk nicotine poisoning to handle a pump you could have operated with one finger."

I sighed, running a hand over my face.

"Well, at least I know why they called it 'self-service.' They weren't kidding."

"You know what, Robert?"

"What?"

"I'm never leaving the Garden State again."

SYD Customer Nightmare*

The heat hit me first. A dry, fierce blast that instantly threatened to melt the temporal adhesives holding my human moustache in place.

"This is Earth sector, specifically the Australian continent, Glarg," I whispered through my comms unit, adjusting my projector. My human disguise, "Gary P. Throckmorton," was wearing a sensible linen shirt. Glarg's, however, was in overly bright turquoise board shorts, an unbuttoned floral shirt, and a hat that featured dangly corks.

"G'day, mate!" Glarg boomed, attempting an accent he'd clearly learned from a vintage 1980s sitcom. "Crikey, it's a stunner!"

I pinched the bridge of my holographic nose.

"We're not here for a holiday, Glarg. We are here to observe the terrestrial energy grids. Just follow my lead, keep your particle emitter quiet, and for the love of the Great Galactic Nebula, do not mention the cheese."

We shuffled along the customs line.

The airport was clean, bright, and plastered with signs warning against bringing in everything from soil to seeds to unapproved meats.

This place was obsessed with biosecurity.

When I reached the counter, the customs officer, a bloke named Dazza, gave me a tired look.

"Passport and arrival card, mate."

I presented the documents.

"Gary P. Throckmorton. Visiting for a geological survey and light sightseeing of the famous 'Outback'."

"Right. Anything to declare, Gary?" Dazza tapped his fingers on the desk. "Foods, plants, animal products, geological samples, anything that might harbour foreign biological contaminants?"

I leaned in conspiratorially.

"Absolutely not, officer. Everything is synthetic, sterilised, and purely for personal consumption. My bag contains only clothes and my personal energy rectifier."

Dazza nodded, about to wave me through.

Then, Glarg, right behind me, leaned over the partition.

"He lies, Dazza!" Glarg cheerfully informed the officer.

"He has the cheese! The purple, pulsating, slightly sentient nutritional gel-cube! It's delicious, but it tried to escape the cargo hold three times during the hyper-jump!"

Dazza's eyes widened to the size of two saucers.

He immediately slammed a large red rubber stamp onto my arrival card, and the surrounding air started beeping furiously.

"Quarantine!" Dazza yelled, pointing a stern finger at Glarg.

"Purple. Pulsating. Sentient. That ticks every box, mate. Step over to the biosecurity check. Immediately."

"But it's just a snack!" Glarg protested, pulling the aforementioned purple, pulsating cube from his shorts pocket.

It briefly emitted a high-pitched, indignant whine.

"That 'snack' is currently classified as an unknown biological entity and a potential threat to our ecosystem!" Dazza declared, ushering us toward a side room. "We can't have unapproved alien flora infecting the Great Barrier Reef, can we?"

As we were led away, Glarg looked genuinely confused.

"I don't understand, Zorp. On Xylar 7, if your cheese tries to escape, they just give it a bigger cage! That's called being accommodating!"

I just rubbed my aching holographic temples.

This was going to be a long trip.

At least the quarantine room had air conditioning.

The air conditioning was the one true positive, a delightful relief from the hostile, solar-flared outdoor climate. We were directed to a sterile stainless-steel table. The purple cheese cube, having been placed in a clear plastic specimen container, pulsed softly under the bright overhead lights.

A new agent, who introduced himself simply as "Bruce from Biosecurity," approached the table wearing thick, bright yellow gloves. He looked like he'd handled much stranger things than a sentient dairy product. He held a small handheld scanner near the container.

"Right-o," Bruce said, his voice flat. "Let's see what we've got here. Looks like high-energy readings... definitely non-terrestrial in origin. And what's this? Is it trying to sing?"

The cheese cube emitted a series of rapid, high-pitched blips and boops.

"That, good sir, is the Xylarian national anthem," Glarg proudly declared, folding his arms. "It only sings when it feels threatened or when it's anticipating a good 'taco' (his pronunciation was still terrible). We call him Reginald."

Bruce slowly lowered the scanner, his moustache twitching. "Reginald. Right. Well, Reginald is being seized under Section 3, Subsection B of the Biosecurity Act: 'Items capable of causing existential chaos to Australian native fauna'."

"Existential chaos?" I exclaimed, temporarily dropping my 'Gary P. Throckmorton,' calmness. "It's a source of Vitamin Q-4! It just needs to be fed every three hours!"

Glarg, ever helpful, decided to demonstrate the feeding process by pulling a tiny, luminous green spatula from his cork hat and attempting to open the plastic container. "He prefers to be spoon-fed, Bruce, old mate!"

"Don't touch the specimen!" Bruce roared, jumping back. "You don't know what kind of spores that thing might drop!"

Glarg huffed. "Spores? It only drops the occasional small, perfectly formed, crystalline sphere of pure joy! Here, catch!" Before Bruce could stop him, Glarg flicked one sphere across the room. It bounced off the wall, hit a power socket, and caused half the lights in the room to flicker violently and the smoke alarm to emit a single, mournful chirp.

"See?" Glarg said, looking triumphant, as Bruce frantically backed away to grab a fire extinguisher. "Pure joy!"

I closed my eyes and wished for the sweet, silent vacuum of deep space. I knew then that getting a cup of the terrestrial beverage known as 'coffee,' let alone observing their electrical grids, was going to require far more temporal displacement than my tiny personal rectifier could manage. We hadn't even made it past the airport's first dimensional layer.

*Dear Reader, if you have been through customs at Sydney International Airport, then you will appreciate this story. I have done this frequently during my working years and later when I moved to Australia, and it has not changed. So, if you travel to OZ, follow the rules and make sure you read and mark all the questions correctly – if you run into trouble, just ring me on 0402-984-086 and I will bail you out.

Discussion in the Breakroom

When people picture NASA, they imagine gleaming rockets, zero-gravity labs, and genius scientists discussing the future of humanity.

In reality? We argue about who finished the last donut.

That's how my morning began—standing in front of an empty pastry box — when Dr. Rick "Kangaroo" Mallory, our token Australian astrophysicist, walked in carrying a mug that said E=MC-G'DAY.

"Mate," he said, peering over my shoulder, "if that's the last cruller gone, I'm filing an interdepartmental grievance."

I sighed. "Blame Jenkins in propulsion. He claims donuts improve his thrust calculations."

Rick nodded solemnly. "That checks out. Sugar's just rocket fuel for humans."

We'd both been up all-night analysing data from the Perseverance 2 rover—Mars's latest overachieving robot, which had just found something shaped suspiciously like a fossilised shrimp.

"So," Rick said, pouring burnt coffee that tasted like despair, "you think we found life on Mars or what?"

I shrugged. "It's probably a rock shaped like a shrimp."

He squinted at me. "That's what they said about Elvis on that tortilla and look how that turned out."

"Rick," I said, "there's no way life started on Mars. Conditions were awful. Radiation, cold, no proper tacos. Life evolved here. On Earth."

He grinned. "You Yanks always think you're the centre of the universe."

"Because we have evidence," I shot back. "Earth has oceans, oxygen, Wi-Fi—everything needed for intelligent life."

Rick sipped his coffee. "And yet, somehow, Congress still exists."

Touché.

We moved to the data screens in the lab, surrounded by blinking monitors and the soft hum of climate-control systems set permanently to Antarctic Penguin Mode.

Rick pulled up the image of the shrimp-rock. "Look at that beauty. You can't tell me this isn't a fossil."

I zoomed in. "I'm telling you it's a potato chip someone dropped in the clean room before launch."

He gasped. "Blasphemy. You think we contaminated Mars with snacks?"

"Wouldn't be the first time," I said. "Remember the cookie crumbs on the Hubble lens?"

Rick wagged his finger. "Nah, mate. Life started on Mars, then hitched a ride here on a meteorite. We're all Martians. Red dust in our veins."

I laughed. "If that's true, explain why I sunburn in fifteen minutes and can't grow potatoes."

"Poor adaptation," he said confidently. "Evolution's slow."

"Rick," I said, "this theory has more holes than the ozone layer you guys punched over Sydney."

That's when Dr. Leopold Finn entered the room.

Finn was new—pale, quiet, with a strange way of blinking slightly out of sync, like his eyelids were on separate Wi-Fi connections. He wore lab goggles even when not needed, and his ID badge photo looked like it was taken under duress.

"Morning, gentlemen," he said in his crisp, odd accent no one could quite place. "Discussing the Martian origins of life again?"

Rick smirked. "Yeah, mate. I say we're cosmic imports. Alex here thinks we're locally grown."

Finn tilted his head. "You are both mistaken."

"Oh?" I asked. "You got a better theory?"

"Yes," he said calmly. "Life began on Mars."

Rick grinned triumphantly. "Ha! Told ya!"

Finn continued, "And I would know—because I was there."

We both froze.

"Sorry," I drawled. "You were where?"

"Mars," he said matter-of-factly. "I was born there. Roughly 4.2 billion years ago."

Rick laughed so hard that he spilled his coffee. "Good one, Leo. You're telling me you're a Martian fossil with a PhD?"

"Not fossil," Finn corrected. "Survivor."

Rick and I exchanged glances; the universal look scientists give each other when deciding whether to call security or record the data.

"Dr. Finn," I said cautiously, "are you feeling, okay? Long hours, maybe too much caffeine?"

"I do not require caffeine," he said. "My metabolism converts solar energy directly."

"Like a plant?" Rick asked.

"More efficiently," Finn said. "I photosynthesize through my epidermis."

I blinked. "So... you're telling us you're solar-powered."

"Precisely."

Rick crossed his arms. "Prove it, sunshine."

Without hesitation, Finn rolled up his sleeve. His skin shimmered faintly greenish, almost metallic. The overhead light flickered. The air smelled faintly of ozone and peppermint.

I gasped. "What the—did you just glow?"

Finn smiled. "A mild photosynthetic reaction. Quite harmless."

Rick leaned closer. "Are you wearing glow-in-the-dark lotion or something?"

Finn's pupils dilated horizontally—horizontally.

Rick jumped back. "Crikey! His eyes did the slidey thing!"

"I assure you," Finn said calmly, "there is no danger. I merely wished to confirm my statement."

I rubbed my temples. "Okay. Let's pretend we believe you. You're saying you're... from Mars. You came here billions of years ago."

"Correct," he said. "My species-initiated panspermia—the seeding of life across suitable planets. Earth was promising. Warm, wet, full of potential."

Rick whistled. "So basically, you're the universe's gardener."

Finn nodded. "And you are our finest bloom."

"That's flattering," I said weakly, "but we've had some pruning issues—politics, reality TV, TikTok..."

Finn sighed. "Yes, our experiment has... deviated."

Rick squinted. "So why reveal yourself now, mate?"

Finn shrugged. "The shrimp fossil. It was one of our pets. I felt nostalgic."

Rick turned to me, whispering, "Do we call security or David Attenborough?"

But before I could respond, Finn reached into his coat pocket and produced a small metallic cube. "Behold," he said.

The cube floated.

"Whoa," Rick breathed. "Anti-gravity tech!"

"Quantum stabilization field," Finn corrected. "My lunchbox."

The cube unfolded like origami, revealing a small, glowing sphere pulsing with light.

Rick's jaw dropped. "What is that?!"

"A culture sample," Finn said. "Pure Martian bioplasm."

"Looks like lime Jell-O," I muttered.

Finn smiled faintly. "It contains the genetic precursors of all life on Earth. I can show you the match."

He tapped the sphere. A holographic DNA helix appeared, spinning lazily above the table. Lines of code connected the Martian sequence to a strand labelled Homo sapiens.

Rick squinted. "So, you're saying we share DNA with Martian goo?"

Finn nodded. "Technically, you are Martian goo—just better dressed."

We stood in stunned silence until Rick burst out laughing. "Well, bloody hell. That explains my sunburn!"

Finn tilted his head. "Indeed. Your species' epidermal design is... inefficient."

I leaned forward. "So, if you've been here this whole time, why stay hidden?"

Finn sighed. "Do you have any idea how difficult it is to file immigration paperwork when you predate borders?"

Rick slapped the table, roaring. "He's got a point, mate. Imagine the visa interview: 'Purpose of visit?'—'Seeding intelligent life.'"

"Length of stay?" "Several billion years!"

We both laughed so hard that we wheezed. Finn simply smiled, glowing faintly like a smug Christmas ornament.

When we finally caught our breath, I said, "So what now? Are you planning to phone home?"

Finn shook his head. "Communication is unnecessary. The network is already active."

"The what now?" Rick asked.

Before we could blink, every monitor in the lab flickered. The NASA logo turned crimson. The shrimp fossil appeared on screen—except now it was... moving.

Rick gulped. "Uh, is it waving?"

Finn nodded. "They've received my signal. They're pleased Earth life has thrived. They may visit soon."

"Visit?" I repeated weakly.

"Yes. To see how the garden's grown."

Rick grinned nervously. "Hope they like weeds."

Finn smiled. "They will be... fascinated."

With that, he picked up his cube, tucked it neatly into his coat, and walked out, humming what sounded suspiciously like Waltzing Matilda.

Rick and I sat in silence.

Finally, he said, "So... you still think life started on Earth?"

I stared at the empty doorway. "I think I need a new theory—and a donut."

He nodded. "And maybe a helmet. In case the gardeners come back."

We looked at each other, then at the glowing shrimp fossil on the monitor, which winked.

Rick muttered, "Crikey. We're so fired."

Waiting

Liam adjusted his chair across the desk from Dr. Elara Vance. Her office was a cozy catastrophe of books, and the scent of aged paper and Earl Grey tea was his favourite cologne. He was ostensibly here to discuss his thesis on 19th-century poetic metre, but the conversation had, conveniently for him, drifted.

Dr. Vance, elegant and sharp in a navy blazer, leaned back.

"So, Liam, you were telling me about your personal collection. Not of rare editions, but of words. Your 'Beautiful Five,' you called them."

Liam felt his pulse quicken, a predictable reaction to her proximity and the directness of her gaze. He gripped his pen a little tighter. "Yes, Doctor. I find that the most beautiful words aren't just phonetic wonders; they're concepts we can only ever aspire to."

"A worthy metric," she murmured, encouraging him. "Begin."

"The first," Liam said, meeting her eyes, "is a cynosure."

Dr. Vance paused, a faint, intellectual smile touching her lips. "A brilliant choice. The definition, please?"

"It is literally the constellation Ursa Minor, the pole star. But metaphorically, it means an object of attention or admiration; something that serves as a focal point or a guide," he explained, meticulously avoiding the actual application of the word to the woman seated opposite him. "I find it beautiful because it represents an absolute certainty in a chaotic sky. A fixed point of wonder."

"Admirable," she conceded, making a minor note on a pad. "A fixed point of wonder can be a dangerous thing, Mr Davies. It sometimes distracts from the journey. And your second?"

"My second is Aurora," Liam continued, letting the syllables roll softly.

"The dawn. The spectacular light displays visible in Earth's upper atmosphere. Its beauty is not just in colour, but in promise. It's a visual declaration that no matter how long the night is, things start over, spectacularly, and always with light."

He observed her.

Her expression remained politcly academic, though she paused, running a finger along the spine of a book.

"An excellent pairing with cynosure, suggesting guidance leading to light," Dr. Vance observed. "You're building a poetic system, Mr Davies. A very hopeful one."

Liam blushed but pressed on.

"Next is sequoia. It sounds so grounded, so ancient, and yet so alive. A word for a tree that simply refuses to die, standing monumentally for centuries. It suggests depth, endurance, and a refusal to be fleeting. It's what I aspire to in... in my convictions."

She nodded, tapping her pen against the notepad.

"Depth and endurance. I appreciate your love of the monumental. Now, for your penultimate choice—before the grand finale."

Her casual reference to the "grand finale" made his throat momentarily dry. He took a nervous sip of cold coffee and prepared his strongest volley.

"My penultimate choice, Doctor, is serendipity."

"Ah, the pleasant accident," Dr. Vance said, her eyes finally leaving the notepad to look directly at him, with a slight lift in one eyebrow. "The discovery of something good or agreeable while not seeking it. Why is that beautiful?"

Liam leaned forward just slightly. "Because it implies that the best things in life are unearned, unexpected, and utterly dependent on chance. It's the word that justifies all the wasted time and wrong turns. It's the sudden, perfect alignment of two entirely separate worlds. It's the meeting of two minds over a dusty, forgotten topic."

He held her gaze, the word serendipity hanging in the air between them.

Dr. Vance's faint smile returned, but this time it held a knowing sharpness.

"And that last definition—'the meeting of two minds over a dusty, forgotten topic'—you've given it a very specific, present-day relevance, haven't you, Mr Davies?" she challenged softly.

There was a long, charged silence, broken only by the distant sounds of students rushing to lectures. Dr. Vance finally placed her pen down deliberately.

"But you only have four," she said, her voice dropping to an almost confidential pitch. "What is your most beautiful word? The one that encapsulates everything you truly seek?"

Liam inhaled slowly.

He had saved this one, the grand prize, for the end.

He knew the risks.

The word was profound, intimate, and entirely too close to home.

"It is eudaemonia," he stated.

"It's not mere happiness. It's human flourishing, Doctor. It's the state of living well, of having a good, fulfilling spirit. It is the highest form of well-being, achieved through rational activity and virtue. A life fully realised."

He paused, his careful academic mask finally slipping to reveal the earnestness beneath.

"And I believe that the path to eudaemonia is often illuminated by a cynosure."

Dr. Vance stood up slowly, her movements deliberate.

She gazed at him for a moment longer than necessary, a professional second too long, before turning and pulling a book from the shelf behind her.

She did not open it.

"Mr Davies," she said, her voice back to its usual crispness, though her cheeks were slightly flushed. "That is a truly beautiful collection of concepts. But I must caution you: the path to eudaemonia requires courage, sometimes more than it does guidance."

She met his eyes, her expression now a perfect, unreadable blend of the academic and the intimate.

"Now, if we don't return to the 19th-century poets immediately, I believe this discussion will have deviated too far from the cynosure of your studies."

Liam smiled, a genuine, private smile that crinkled the corners of his eyes, and exhaled softly, barely audible. "I want you, body and soul," he whispered, not realising the depth of the charged silence had allowed the words to carry clearly across the short distance.

Dr. Vance's smile did not falter, but a sudden, new tension settled in her shoulders. She turned back to the desk, running her finger over a leather-bound spine.

"Waiting," she said, her voice quiet, soft but encouraging, "is also a great and beautiful word, Liam."

Agent 9 Reports

My designation is Agent 9, Field Investigator, 3rd Class, reporting directly to the Martian High Council on Planetary Assimilation.

I am currently operating under a deep-cover persona, "Joaquín Fernández Fiqueroa de la Cruz," in the specific area designated Target Zone 7, Sector Cienfuegos, Cuba, on the planet Earth.

My mission began, as all truly great endeavours do, with a profound neural calibration shock.

One moment, I was simply Joaquín, sweating under the unforgiving Cuban sun, attempting to convince my genetically inferior, four-legged terrestrial transport unit, a donkey named Fidel, to haul a new load of mangoes.

The next, a blinding, white-hot flash of pure, unadulterated consciousness erupted behind my left optic nerve, courtesy of Fidel's surprisingly robust hind hoof, delivered directly to my cranium. The sound was like a thousand distant Martian seismic drills starting up all at once.

The moment my body impacted the dusty earth, the thick, cumbersome veil of Terran identity (Joaquín, mangoes, mortgage, coño) dissolved.

I remembered everything.

I was not a humble farmer; I was Agent 9.

I had been embedded here for two solar cycles, patiently waiting for the signal, which, in a brilliant move of stealth coding by the High Council, was apparently the concussion administered by a Sub-Sentient Terrestrial Transport Unit (SSTTU).

Ingenious.

I rose, brushing dust and what I recognised as primitive brain-matter-stabilization-residue from my trousers. The pain in my head was acceptable; it was merely the cooling process of the implanted data chip.

I looked at Fidel, who was now grazing placidly.

"You have served your purpose, SSTTU-Fidel," I declared, my voice now carrying the low, resonant, and utterly authoritative frequency of a Martian Field Agent. "Your termination protocol is pending, but for now, you remain a necessary piece of planetary camouflage. Remain docile."

The burro just flicked an ear.

Clearly, it was highly motivated by fear.

Excellent.

I retreated to my Observation Post Alpha-4, which the Terran locals refer to as a "casita." I immediately began analysing my operational base.

The structure is made of porous, sun-baked clay and corrugated metal—shockingly poor insulation, showing a serious lack of geothermal management infrastructure on this planet.

My primary task was to decode the "mission objectives."

According to the internal chronometer, I was running two subjective Terran hours behind schedule. I found the mission data scroll jammed into the magnetic message receiver, a primitive, carved wooden box hanging near the door.

I unfolded the thick, fibrous parchment.

The message was encrypted using a local dialect known as "Handwriting-of-Wife," a common, irritatingly complex Terran cipher.

The instructions were:

1. Acquire energy source: paquete de arroz (rice, one bag. Must be a compact, granular fuel source for the Assimilation Drones.).

2. Then acquire nutrient paste: frijoles negros (black beans, essential protein, and pigment base for the new High Council uniform fabric).

3. Then acquire a stabilising agent: un litro de Ron (one litre of Rum, a crucial solvent for lubricating the gravity stabilisers). And perhaps a small personal calibration dose for the Agent.

4. Finally, I needed to acquire the security asset: No olvides la bolsa de pan (Don't forget the bag of bread). (The High Council must be serious; they want me to secure a terrestrial weapon—a "baguette bomb," perhaps? I will investigate the tactical use of stale bread.)

I meticulously transferred the objectives to my neural display pad (the palm of my hand, where I keep scratching the mosquito bites).

Now I was to execute Phase One: Resource Acquisition and Local Population Assessment.

I donned my most convincing disguise: a bright, sweat-stained cotton shirt, short pants, and the Terran footwear known as chancletas (which I theorize are used to ward off floor-based predators).

Stepping outside, I immediately encountered a Prime Indigenous Specimen (P.I.S.), an elderly female designated "Abuela Elena," tending to a flowering bush. She was a known node of information transmission.

"Joaquín, mi alma," she greeted me, her voice a low, gravelly Terran rumble. "What happened to your head? It looks like Fidel tried to crack a coconut on it."

I activated my truth-matrix filter. "A mere atmospheric irregularity, Elena. Tell me, what is the current Planetary Defence Readiness Level (PDRL)?"

She blinked, wiping a bead of sweat from her upper lip.

"The level of defence? Ay, Dios mío. Well, they are out of milk at the bodega, and the rooster next door did not crow this morning. The PDRL is looking low, I think."

Excellent! The Terrans communicate their readiness levels via mundane shortages and poultry failures! Simple yet brilliant deception.

"And the local population's mood?"

I pressed, leaning in conspiratorially. "Are they prepared for a rapid, structural, and complete geopolitical transition?"

She sighed, fanning herself with a woven palm leaf.

"They are prepared for the baseball game tonight, and they are prepared for a strong cafecito. That is all anyone ever prepares for, mi cielo."

Cafecito! A potent terrestrial mind-control agent.

I made a mental note: Martian invasion must be scheduled after the midday cafecito intake, or risk a sudden, jittery, over-caffeinated counterattack.

"Thank you, P.I.S.-Elena. Your cooperation in this pre-invasion diagnostic survey will be noted favourably."

"You are a strange boy, Joaquín," she muttered, returning to her bush. "Go get your rice before the place closes."

The bodega, a small, brightly painted concrete structure, was the designated Resource Exchange Nexus. Inside, the air conditioning was non-existent, and the Nexus Operator, a man named Tío Ramón, was asleep on a stool.

I approached the counter with purpose.

"Nexus Operator Ramón," I stated, projecting Martian authority.

"I require a rapid deployment of the granular fuel source (rice), the protein paste (black beans), and the solvent (rum). Quantify the transactional unit in the local currency."

Ramón didn't open his eyes. "Joaquín, stop talking like you swallowed a dictionary. You owe me eighty pesos from last week. And tell your wife to stop sending you for rum so early."

"The rum is not for recreational intake, Terran! It is for the stabilization of gravitational displacement fields!"

Ramón squinted one eye open, examining my forehead.

"Did Fidel finally win the argument? You've got a lump on your head the size of a pigeon egg, muchacho."

I ignored the reference to my neural calibration shock.

I located the target items. The rice was stacked in brittle paper bags; the black beans were in a clear, labelled container. The rum was, miraculously, exactly where it needed to be.

The security asset (bread) was the last hurdle.

Ramón pointed to a glass case containing a long, crusty loaf.

"I must analyse this weapon," I said, picking up the loaf gingerly. It was surprisingly light, brittle, and had an unusual texture. "What is the maximum effective blast radius of this baguette bomb?"

Ramón began laughing, a loud, wheezing, uncontrolled sound that showed low intelligence. "The only thing that bread blasts is garlic butter! It's just bread, mi hijo. You eat it."

Deception! I realised.

The Terrans hide their most potent bioweapon in plain sight, masquerading it as a foodstuff. They had successfully infiltrated my previous Terran personality. I would not fall for it again. I secured the bread, placing it carefully in my acquisition sack alongside the rum, rice, and beans.

Back at Observation Post Alpha-4, I organised the acquired assets.

Everything was in place.

The data was conclusive: Earth's defence strategy was based on confusion, slowness, short supplies, and aggressive consumption of high-caffeine and high-alcohol beverages. A standard pre-assimilation scenario.

Now, for the final report to the High Council. How to transmit the data?

My portable transmission unit (my cell phone) was currently out of power, having been used by the former Joaquín to watch blurry baseball highlights.

I scanned the environment.

Ah, yes.

The coconut.

A perfect, naturally occurring hard-shell satellite dish, common in this sector.

I climbed onto the roof of the casita (a structurally dubious undertaking, but a necessary risk), holding the coconut high. I began my uplink transmission, speaking clearly into the fibre-covered surface, certain my voice was being converted into subspace Martian-band frequencies.

"High Council, this is Agent 9, reporting from Target Zone 7. The mission is a preliminary success. Planetary defences are minimal. Their weapons, codenamed 'baguette bombs,' are structurally unstable and prone to crumbling. I feel that their fundamental weakness is a deep-seated cultural dependency on a potent mind-altering drug, 'Rum,' and a neural depressant known as 'siesta.' My opinion is that for the conquest of Earth to succeeds we must execute the invasion by deploying the invasion force precisely at 2:00 PM Terran Time. This is the optimal window, as the indigenous population will be heavily sedated and unable to mount a coordinated defence. The immediate priority upon landing is to secure all coffee-making apparatus to prevent a coordinated cafecito-fuelled counter-revolution."

"The SSTTU-Fidel is still functional, though emotionally volatile. It is currently being utilised as an antenna base. I require immediate extraction, primarily because the heat management system of my deep-cover uniform is failing, and I have a significant craving for a cold Cerveza Cristal."

"Agent 9, standing by for Assimilation Order. Victory for Mars. Glory to the High Council. And please send a large bag of ice."

I placed the coconut down carefully, satisfied.

I had done my part.

The conquest of Earth, starting right here in Cienfuegos, was imminent.

All I had to do now was wait for the mothership.

In the meantime, I had a bag of rice, some beans, a bottle of solvent, and a weaponised loaf of bread. A quick calculation showed that a small personal dose of the gravitational solvent was perfectly acceptable, given the stress of command.

I took the bottle of rum, sat down in the blistering sun, and patiently awaited my promotion.

The Big Crush

Professor Eloise Hart had taught cosmology for twelve years and survived every variety of conspiracy theory, caffeine-fuelled epiphany, and student who believed YouTube counted as peer-reviewed research.

But nothing quite prepared her for Max Turner, her overly enthusiastic and possibly lovesick third-year student.

That morning, she was mid-lecture when Max's hand shot up so fast it created a small gust of wind.

"Yes, Mr Turner?" She asked, chalk still hovering over the word Singularity.

"Professor Hart," he said earnestly, "I think the Big Bang theory is wrong."

Eloise smiled.

"Many physicists have proposed alternatives, Mr Turner. Which one are you referring to?"

He puffed out his chest like a man about to challenge Einstein to arm-wrestling. "The Big Bounce."

"The Big Bounce," she repeated.

"As in, the idea that the universe didn't begin from nothing but collapsed and re-expanded?"

"Exactly! It's a cosmic boomerang. A universe with rhythm!" He grinned. "Unlike my dancing."

The class chuckled. Eloise tried not to.

"That's an interesting way to put it."

Max leaned forward, eyes gleaming.

"Think about it, Professor. Expansion, contraction, expansion. Over and over. The universe breathes. It's like cosmic yoga!"

"Cosmic yoga," Eloise muttered, rubbing her temple.

"So, according to you, the cosmos does a downward dog?"

"Well, not literally," Max said. "But if space-time stretches and compresses, who's to say it's not limber?"

The class erupted again.

Eloise sighed, pretending to adjust her glasses, so no one saw her smile.

Max had a rare quality in students: equal parts curiosity and chaos.

"Mr Turner," she said, "while the Big Bounce is a valid hypothesis, we still lack observational evidence. The Big Bang remains our best model."

He frowned.

"Evidence, yes, but it's incomplete. Besides, a Bang sounds so abrupt. Bouncing feels more hopeful. Gentler. More alive."

"Physics," she reminded him, "is not about emotional preference."

"Still," he said dreamily, "a universe that bounces back instead of dying out, it's romantic, don't you think?"

Eloise blinked. "Romantic?"

"Sure! It means every ending is just another beginning. Like, say, a, uh, brilliant, unattainable professor's heart were broken by a, let us say, a mysterious student, the cosmos itself would tell him to try again."

The class went still.

Eloise froze, chalk mid-air. "Mr Turner," she said, clearing her throat, "the laws of thermodynamics do not comment on your love life."

A girl in the back whispered, "Oh, they will now."

After class, Max lingered as the others filed out.

"Professor Hart?" he said shyly. "Sorry if I made things awkward. I just, well, I find you... inspiring."

Eloise smiled kindly.

"That's very flattering, Mr Turner. But perhaps focus your inspiration on your thesis."

He nodded rapidly.

"Right. My thesis. I'm calling it The Universe: A Rebounding Relationship."

She stifled a laugh. "Catchy."

He hesitated. "Would you ever, um, discuss it over coffee?"

"Your thesis?"

"Yes! And possibly other topics that also involve quantum entanglement... metaphorically speaking."

Eloise tilted her head. "Mr Turner, are you asking me on an academic date?"

He turned red.

"No! I mean—yes? I mean—coffee purely for intellectual stimulation. Unless you'd prefer emotional stimulation. Wait. That sounded wrong."

"Max," she said gently, "take a deep breath before you implode."

He did. Loudly.

"Tell you what," she said. "If your final paper convincingly argues for the Big Bounce using solid data, not just charm, I'll buy you that coffee. Deal?"

He straightened. "Deal! Prepare to be cosmically persuaded."

Two weeks later, his paper landed on her desk. The title read:

"Love and the Expanding Universe: Why Everything Deserves a Second Chance."

It was equal parts physics, poetry, and unfiltered devotion. He'd even written an equation that simplified to:

$$E = MC^2 + YOU.$$

Eloise laughed so hard she nearly spilled her tea.

At the bottom he'd scribbled, P.S. Even the universe couldn't resist bouncing back to you.

She wrote one comment in red ink:

Grade: A-minus. (Points deducted for romantic inflation.)

Coffee at 4?

When Max showed up at the café, he was beaming. "So," he said, sliding into the seat opposite her, "what changed your mind?"

Eloise smiled over her cup.

"Maybe the Big Bang isn't the only explosive idea in the universe."

About the Author

The Cuban Revolution in 1959 presented José with one of his many life challenges. José was born in La Habana; Cuba, and the Cuban Revolution saw him get on a plane alone at eleven years of age and arrive at an orphanage in the small town of Washington, Georgia. He did not get to see his parents again until he was eighteen years old and had graduated from high school in Atlanta, Georgia.

He studied Business Administration at Georgia State University. From university, he headed into the finance world working for the First National Bank of Atlanta (now Wells Fargo) and then moved into the financial consulting world working as a project manager, travelling to many assignments in the United States, Europe, and Australia.

When José is not writing, you can find him sitting at the local shopping centre watching people and getting inspiration for his future characters.

When not in front of his computer working away, José is reading or spending time on leisurely walks around the Camden area.

Of course, your comments, and reviews are always welcome.

Please visit https://jfnodar.com.au/book-reviews/ and let me know what you thought of this book of short stories and poetry.

Good, bad, or indifferent, I will always welcome your honest opinion.

Send me an email at info@jfnodar.com.au

Thank you for your purchase!

Other books by José F. Nodar:

English

Books, Pens & Larceny
Mending Hearts at Crystal Cove
A Love Finally Spoken
The Ghost Detective's First Case
The Compass Legacy
The Teacher's Assistant
A Night of Love
The Universe Between Us
The Time Bus
SEX
Stories to Share with My Partner Book 1
Stories to Share with My Partner Book 2
Stories to Share with My Partner Book 3
Stories to Share with My Partner Book 4
Stories to Share with My Partner Book 5
Stories to Share with My Partner Book 6
Stories to Share with My Partner Book 7
Stories to Share with My Partner Book 8
Stories to Share with My Partner Book 9
Stories to Share with My Partner Book 10

Spanish

Cuentos Para Compartir con Mi Pareja Libro 1
Cuentos Para Compartir con Mi Pareja Libro 2
Cuentos Para Compartir con Mi Pareja Libro 3
Libros, Bolígrafos y Hurto
Reparando Corazones en Crystal Cove
Un Amor Expresado
El Autobús del Tiempo